I0726166

House of Poetry

and other stories

House of Poetry
and other stories

Lawrence Reid Bechtel

POCAHONTAS PRESS
DUBLIN, VA

House of Poetry
and other stories

Copyright © 2022 by Lawrence Reid Bechtel

ISBN 13: 978-1-955338-04-2

Cover & interior designs by Deborah Warren
Cover photo courtesy of David Bellinger
Printed in the United States of America

POCAHONTAS PRESS

DUBLIN, VA
POCAHONTASPRESS.COM

This book is dedicated to Teague Stefan Bechtel, Rose Shawhan, and Haley Jayne Bechtel.

Foreword

Welcome, Dear Reader! You can expect variety from the stories which follow. They were written--and rewritten, some of them several times--over a span of sixteen years, 2004-2020. The earliest are "The Rhino in the Garden," and "Drawing Rizelda," which emerged from my story-telling days at the Blacksburg New School. "Shine," "Child of God," and "Thorn" are recent, and may become part of another work. I took all of the stories through a rigorous edit based upon lessons learned from a pair of excellent Tinker Mountain Writers Workshops led by Barbara Jones, Executive Editor with Henry Holt & Co. and hosted by Hollins University in 2021.

I wish to thank Becky Cox, who ably proof-read early versions of these stories, and Deborah Warren of Pocahontas Press, for her superb editorial skills and for skillfully guiding this book into print.

I hope you enjoy reading these stories as much as I enjoyed writing them.

Contents

Hitch Up Your Britches

A NEW PLANT MANAGER HAD BEEN HIRED to turn the company around. He spent two weeks, clipboard in hand, observing operations and taking notes. Then he called a staff meeting. Everyone waited uneasily in their seats around the long table until he entered the room. He did not sit. Positioning his large hands to support his weight, he leaned forward menacingly.

"The problem I see," he said, looking slowly around the room, "is *morale*." He waited for this to sink in. "There are a few of us who are—*grumpy bears*." He briefly smiled. "And the grumpiest of our grumpy bears is—you there, in the corner, trying to ignore me, *Fish!*"

At the sound of his hated nickname, Peter Salmon, who had been slouched in his seat, doodling, jerked upright. The pencil flew out of his hand and landed on the table. The plant manager deftly grabbed and snapped it sharply in half. The sound to Peter was like a tree breaking off in a storm. He was sure he would be fired, which would be a royal bitch. Because as much as he hated his job, he was only two years from retirement. He had calculated exactly what his pension would be, but not minus his two best earning years.

Ceremoniously, the plant manager handed the pencil pieces to the man on his right, who passed them on to the next man. Hand to hand they went until the pieces got to Peter, who tried vainly to put them back together.

The plant manager watched him for a moment. "Tomorrow," he said, "at company expense, I will send one of you to the Guiding Light Conference Center for a daylong seminar, *Building a Positive Attitude in the Modern Workplace*. The fortunate individual who is thus chosen shall become our *Ambassador of Enthusiasm*." The plant manager struck the table with his fist. "Who shall be this Ambassador?" He gazed slowly around the room. His eyes settled on Peter. "*You*, Fish."

Everyone turned toward Peter, relieved and shocked.

The meeting adjourned and everyone scuttled from the room, except for Peter, who was cornered by the plant manager, dangling a set of car keys. "Surprised, grumpy bear?"
Peter could have punched him.

The plant manager dropped the keys into Peter's hand. "Do not fail me, my dear Ambassador of Enthusiasm. Return with *words of wisdom*."

No assignment in all his twenty-eight years at the plant so galled Peter as this one. *Ambassador of Enthusiasm. Grumpy bear*. Assinine! He should have walked. Should have thrown down the keys and walked out the door. But there was his pension to consider. If he could endure this prick of a plant manager and his goddamn seminar.

The next morning at the crack of dawn, dressed in his only suit, Peter headed down the road for the Guiding Light Conference Center. Halfway there the engine temp light came on and wisps of smoke issued from under the hood. Trapped in the passing lane by a caravan of trucks, he sped up for two miles before cutting a sharp diagonal across the right lane and up an exit ramp, hoping to find a gas station. A sign, pocked with bullet holes blocked his way at the top: "CONSTRUCTION. NO RE-ENTRY TO INTERSTATE. YOUR TAX DOLLARS AT WORK." There was no gas station.

Smoke was now billowing from under the hood, along with a burnt smell from under the dash. Peter veered around the signs, plunged through a cluster of safety cones, and sped down a gravel road, desperate for help. He zigzagged through a grove of trees, then swung into a blind curve. Meeting him was the huge grill of a rusty pickup truck, topped by a shiny swan with uplifted wings as a hood ornament. Peter had just time to brace himself before the collision. Locked in a steely embrace, the two vehicles slid off the road and down a bank into a swamp thick with cattails. The car hissed like a hot pan. Peter struggled to get out the door, which swung shut on his ankle. He cried out, shoved the door open again, and lunged from the car, falling on all fours in the mud. Furious, he hobbled up to the road.

The driver of the pickup, sunburnt and wrinkled, stood there calmly watching him.

If Peter had not been near panic, he would have asked the old man how in hell he'd gotten out of his truck so fast and up to the road, dry and unmuddied.

Peter pointed at his watch. "Thirty minutes! I got to be at the Guiding Light Conference Center in *thirty minutes*. The goddamn plant manager will kill me if I don't make it!"

The man wiped his brow, struck his chest twice,

drew a cigarette out of his pocket and began smoking.

"Did you hear me? *Thirty minutes!* You hit my car and now look." He pointed to their vehicles, entangled together in the glistening mud. "What am I going to do?"

The man put out the cigarette with his bare fingers and carefully put the long stub in his shirt pocket. "Sometimes," he said, in a gravelly voice, "you got to hitch up your britches an' start walkin'."

"What?"

"We walk on over to that place. You git to your conference, and I call my brother to get my truck out. Plus that tin can of yours."

"Great! How far we got to go?"

"'Bout nine mile."

"Nine miles? I can't walk nine miles!" Peter opened his arms. "Look at me!"

The man studied Peter for a moment. "There is a shortcut."

"Thank God. How short?"

"'Bout three mile."

"That I can maybe handle."

"Jes 'cause it's shorter, don't mean it's easier."

"Shorter's got to be easier. Let's go!"

The man adjusted his hat and thrust out a rough hand. "Alrighty then. Name's Virgil."

Peter extended his own smooth hand. "Peter," he said.

"Mind if I call you *Pete*?"

Peter smiled. "Hell, no!" he said and they shook.

Virgil plunged straight into a bramble patch.

Peter plowed in after him, forcing his way

     House of Poetry

through the thorny, tangled briar stems.

Virgil stopped. "Holler every now and then, Pete. Bears in here."

"Bears?"

Virgil plowed forward.

"Help!" cried Peter, struggling to keep up. "Help!"

"No, Pete! Don't holler 'hep!' Bears might get the wrong idea. Holler 'Shoo bear!'"

"Shoo bear! Oh, bear, *shoo!*"

No bears appeared, but mosquitoes and deer flies did, attacking in force. Between fighting the brambles and the insects, Peter was soon sweating, bloody, and covered in welts. "Virgil! I'm dying of thirst back here! You got any water?"

Virgil stopped, drew a hand across his brow, slapped his chest twice, and lit a cigarette. He parted a curtain of brambles and pointed down a steep bank to a muddy torrent at the bottom.

"Is that drinkable?"

"Depends on how thirsty you are."

"I need a drink, not a dunking!"

"Hold your head up," said Virgil, lifting his chin to illustrate. "And keep moving."

"We've got to cross that?"

"Yep."

"I don't swim very well."

"I don't swim at all!" said Virgil, moving his pack of cigarettes from his shirt pocket to his hat band. He crouched, surfer-style, and pushing off from a tree stump, slalomed down the slick, muddy bank, neatly evading a rock outcrop, and shot into the water. Imitating Virgil's stance, Peter gingerly began his descent.

His feet came out from under him and he began rolling. Clutching desperately at every branch and stone, he hurtled down the slope and plunged headlong into the shockingly cold water. He touched bottom—barely, and went bouncing on tiptoe, struggling against the current, and straining to keep his chin up. Just as he prepared to haul himself onto the far bank, Peter felt the toe of his shoe catch. He tugged awkwardly, slipped underwater, and in desperation jerked his foot loose from the shoe. Struggling up the steep bank and banging his elbow sharply on a rock he finally arrived at the top.

Virgil, dripping wet but unfazed, stood waiting. "That warn't bad," he said, drawing a hand across his brow, slapping his chest twice, and pulling the cigarette pack from his hat.

"Not bad!" said Peter, wringing out his shirt. "I nearly drowned."

"Better than burnin' to death."

Peter rubbed his bare foot, at a loss for words.

Virgil went on smoking. "You ever been through a rhododendron thicket?"

"No," said Peter, examining a cut on his hand. "But it can't be any worse than what we've been through."

"You might not think so once we in it," said Virgil, as he took a last drag on his cigarette. He ducked low into a complicated jungle of twisting branches hung with glossy leaves shining like lanterns. Ducking, crawling, falling, Peter battled his way through the tangle of branches trying to keep Virgil in sight. At last, hot, bruised, and panting for air, he limped into a stony clearing.

     House of Poetry

Virgil wiped his brow, slapped his chest twice, and lit a cigarette.

Peter rubbed his bleeding knee. "Why in God's name do you slap your chest like that?"

"Pacemaker!" Pulling back his shirt at the collar, Virgil exposed his neck and shoulder. Just where the skin turned from sunburnt brown to pale white, Peter saw the clear outlines of a small box, about two inches square, under his skin.

"Goes on the fritz now and again. Gotta slap it back to life."

"That's not good."

"Only got one lung, too."

A terrible premonition overwhelmed Peter: Virgil keeling over dead, leaving Peter lost and alone in this wilderness. "If you've got a pacemaker and only one lung, you shouldn't be smoking those cancer sticks. They'll kill you!"

Virgil sat down on a rock. He picked a strand of tobacco from his lip. "Oh, I already died."

"*Died?*"

"Yep. Ma ol' pumper gave out. Had to fly me down to the big hospital in Roanoke. Died three times on the way. Had me on the operatin' table five hours."

"My God!"

"When I came to the doc said, 'Virgil, a man in your condition ought to be dead. What's your secret?' 'Doc,' I said, 'I don't give a damn. No sir! Don't give a *damn.*'"

Peter threw down the grass stem he was chewing. "What do you mean you don't give a damn! What, are you suicidal?"

Virgil pressed out his cigarette, tore open the

paper, and scattered the tobacco strands. "Pete, I ain't precious about myself and you is."

The remark so stunned Peter he fell back, as if absorbing a punch.

"Copperhead!" yelled Virgil, pointing.

Terrified, Peter jumped.

"'Nother one!"

Peter jumped again.

"A whole nest of 'em!" Virgil cried out, tap-dancing his way deftly from rock to rock to the far edge of the clearing, with Peter in clumsy panic after him. Safe from snakes Peter dropped to the ground and rubbed his bare, bloody foot. He inspected his scratched arms. He rubbed his knee. He swatted at mosquitoes. "Forget about the Guiding Light," he begged. "Get me to a doctor and a hot shower. *Please*!"

"Oh now, Pete! We damn close. Jes need to cross that there little-bitty bog."

It didn't look little-bitty to Peter at all. "Can't we go around?"

"Could. If you don't mind two miles the one way, or three miles t'other." Virgil strode into the bog. "The mud knocks the ticks off."

"Ticks!" exclaimed Peter, pulling up his pant-legs and checking his shins.

"Don't bother, Pete. B'lieve me, you got 'em!"

Peter let go his pantleg, and gingerly stepped into the mud, which oozed up over his toes.

Virgil raised a finger in warning. "Don't get sucked under. If you got to, fall forward and swim!" He demonstrated, with Peter following, despite the stinking mud up his nose. Exhausted, he finally crawled out on the other side.

Virgil was waiting, cigarette in hand. "Lookee there, Pete!"

Peter drew up beside him, putting a hand on Virgil's shoulder to steady himself, and drank in the view: trim, green lawns; manicured flower beds; clusters of tall, sinuous grasses. A winding brick pathway led to a picturesque tile-roofed stone building like something from old Italy. A round tower like a lighthouse, complete with revolving beam of light, flashed its welcome.

Peter broke into a happy, limping shamble.

At that moment, participants in the *Building Enthusiasm in the Modern Workplace* seminar were gathered in the conference sanctuary. The facilitator, a big woman in billowing chiffon, had just then enjoined the group to clasp hands in a "circle of light." She was leading them in a chant: "We feel good! We feel great! We feel terrific!" She encouraged "free form dancing" and hand clapping. Peter, muddy and disheveled, burst through the doors, stumbled into the circle, and collapsed on the floor.

"That there's Pete!" said a raspy voice from the doorway. "Fine fellar. Tough as bull leather. Come through a deal a trouble ta git here!"

The facilitator swept forward, gathered Peter to her ample bosom and followed by her chanting participants carried him into the Wellness Suite, where he was bathed, groomed, massaged, and sprinkled with sweet-smelling oils and unguents.

In the morning he woke from a sound sleep to find a tall man in a bright shirt and unkempt hair seated at his bedside. "So *this* is the 'grumpy bear' I've heard so much about."

Peter almost retorted, "once a grumpy bear, always a grumpy bear." But the smile on his face wouldn't conform to those words. Or any words.

"You don't *seem* very grumpy this morning."

"Just you wait," he might have said. Except for the darn smile, which felt as good on the inside as it apparently looked on the outside.

"In fact," the doctor said, scribbling something on a pad of paper, "I will report that you are positively *transformed*. So I am sending you back in *style*."

Dressed in a white suit with pink tie, Peter Salmon was installed in a stretch limousine. With police escort, and the wrecked company car in tow, he was driven back to the plant. Virgil led the caravan in his old truck, whose ornamental swan with uplifted wings gleamed like a trophy.

The plant manager had been steaming with outrage from the moment he had received a message from the Guiding Light Conference Center alerting him to Peter's "singular courage" and imminent arrival.

A secretary came into his office and leaned over his shoulder. "I think you'll want to come outside and look at this," she whispered.

Frowning, he rose from his seat, and trailed by his staff walked down the corridor and out the front door. There, in the circular drive, next to a white limo flanked by police at attention, a phalanx of motorcycles, and a grizzled man in a rusty truck, stood somebody in a gleaming white suit. His arm was in a sling, and one eye was swelled shut, but he was smiling like a pumpkin.

The plant manager came slowly down the steps. He cocked his head, puzzled. "Fish?" he asked, wrinkling his nose.

"No, sir. *Pete.*"

"Pete?"

"That's right. Your *Ambassador of Enthusiasm.*"

The plant manager ran a hand through his thinning hair.

"Aren't you going to ask me a question?"

"Question?"

"You know. What are my *golden words of wisdom?*"

"Yes," said the plant manager, recovering some of his authority. "Please do tell me your words of wisdom--gained at company expense, my personal endorsement, and your appearance in this ridiculous cavalcade."

Peter took a deep breath and slowly let it out. "I don't give a damn! *No,* sir. I don't give a *damn.*"

The plant manager met Peter's eye. "That's *all?*"

"Oh no!" said Peter, raising a forefinger. "That is *definitely* not all!"

"Well?"

Peter gazed contemplatively at the sky for a moment. "It's like my old friend here taught me," he said, cocking a thumb toward Virgil in his truck, "'sometimes, you got to hitch up your britches and start walkin'.' And *now* is the sometimes for *me.*"

So saying, and despite his bad limp and sore elbow, Pete Salmon sauntered gaily off, singing as he went: "*You got to walk that lonesome valley/You got to walk it by yourself/Nobody here can walk it for you/You got to walk it by yourself . . !*"

Three Liberties

THE GENERAL ROBERT E. LEE MONUMENT would be unveiled in the afternoon, and Shine aimed to do a brisk business from it. People had been coming into town for a week, including a good part of what was left of the rebel army, old men gathering for a last hurrah. Shine had paid a patrolman a full five dollars to move his setup from down on Water Street by the railroad tracks right up to Second Street, across from the park. He had bought on credit from Dickerson's store three tins of polish, one brown, one black, and one amber, at fifty cent each. He had stubbed in fresh bristles to his cleaning brush, sewn a tear in his buffing cloth, waxed his shoeshine box, and spent hours reupholstering The Throne, his name for the customer chair.

Shine borrowed a two-wheeled pushcart to get The Throne into place by noon. He wanted to be up there at ten but the patrolman would not allow it without another five dollars. Even so Shine figured to make a solid twelve dollars, at one dollar per shine, ten minutes per customer, twelve customers in the two hours. With tips he could take home twenty or more. Think of it!

With everything in order, Shine sat down on his shoe-shine box and watched the preparations in the park. A stage was being set up in front and chairs for the dignitaries wheeled in on dollies, with room for the rest of everybody to stand and watch. The monument was hidden under a gigantic flag, the stars and bars. He had heard that General Lee's granddaughter, a girl of three, would pull a cord at the appointed hour and the flag would fall away.

Shine gloated a little. It took nerve for a Black man to be out here in plain view like this, plying his trade. But he had done it. There was not another shoe-shine man, even a white one, anywhere up or down Second. He began earmarking the money he expected to take in: how much to pay down his debt at Dickerson's store, how much to help with the back rent, how much for tar and shingles to fix the roof leak, with still a nickel left over for his own pocket. Twenty or more dollars in no more than two hours was a high goal, but a man had to set high to get high in life, as Uncle Baxter used to say. He, Shine, was there to prove it, this 21st day of May, in the year of Our Lord nineteen hundred and twenty-four.

"Good morning, there, Shine!"

"Good morning, Mr. Foster, sir!" he said, getting at once to his feet. Here he had been daydreaming and already a customer.

Mr. Foster walked with a cane, taking all his weight on one leg and throwing forward the other, back and forth, like a boat in choppy water. The result of shrapnel at Chickamauga, he said, time and again.

"You looking awful fine this morning," said Shine. "You really trimmed out."

Mr. Foster stopped, leaning on his cane with both hands. "Why thank you, Shine. If only the damn shrapnel in my knee would stop acting up. The sur-

 House of Poetry

geon swore he got it all, but I knew better. It was hell at Chickamauga."

"I'm sure it was, Mr. Foster."

"Why you up here on Second Street?"

"Got permission, Mr. Foster, so's to serve fine folks like yourself."

Mr. Foster nodded.

"Say, would you like a shine? I got a special going today. Special shine for a special day." Shine opened his box, and showed the new tins of wax, brown and black and amber, and held up his brush and buffing cloth. "Why don't you set up in The Throne here, Mr. Foster."

Mr. Foster scratched in his beard, which came nearly down to his vest coat pocket. "How much is this special shine going to set me back?"

"One dollar is all, Mr. Foster. Just one dollar."

"One dollar! Who do you think I am, President Coolidge?"

"Oh, Mr. Foster, you better. You a veteran. Got shrapnel in your knee to prove it. Now tell me, Mr. Foster, would you celebrate the monument to General Lee and your shoes not shined? Why, the old gentleman might just roll over in his grave and his horse with him."

Mr. Foster still complained the price was too steep but hoisted himself up in The Throne anyway. "There you go, Shine," he said, breathing hard. "Give me the special."

Shine opened the new tin of brown and went to work, first on the toe box scuffs. Stitching was tore some at the welt, and the left heel was wore down, no doubt from the way Mr. Foster rolled his weight. But

Shine, he would bring up these shoes to look almost like new. Polish the sole edge, too. Customers always liked that touch.

Another man came up, also with a long beard. "Foster!" said the man. "I thought you must be in the grave by now."

"Hornbeam! You're one to talk."

"I'm here, ain't I?"

They bantered back and forth about Chickamauga and ribbed each other over who was first to break through the gap under Longstreet. They both had run out of ammunition and begun pitching spent mini balls in close. "And goddamn if we didn't nearly starve afterwards," said Hornbeam.

"We'd have won the war," said Mr. Foster, "if we'd a-had the rations those Yanks had."

Shine was just finishing. Working the two ends of his buffing cloth at once, he came around the horn, as he called the heel, swung forward along both shanks, and then slid down across the toe box. "There you go!" he said, sitting back so the shoes could be in full view.

Mr. Foster turned his shoes this way and that, nodding with approval. "Fine! Mighty fine. You're a magician, Shine." He turned to his friend. "Say Hornbeam, you best set in here now and get yourself a shine. You don't want to go in shameful to see the General, do you?"

"I give you a special, too, Mr. Hornbeam, good as Mr. Foster here. Prob'ly they put you two right up there on the podium, your shoes look so good."

Mr. Foster lowered himself with difficulty from The Throne, and Hornbeam, still agile for an old man, scrambled up in the seat after him.

   House of Poetry

"That will be one dollar, Mr. Foster."

Mr. Foster turned to Hornbeam. "What say we toss a coin when Shine is done? Whoever loses, pays both." They accused each other of being cheats and liars who could not be trusted, but finally agreed.

Shine would rather have had money in his pocket from Mr. Foster, and then money in his pocket from this Hornbeam. But both men were well dressed and ought to be trustworthy, he thought, Mr. Foster especially. So he went to work on Hornbeam's shoes, which were amber in tone, so he opened the amber tin to match. These shoes were quality, with stitching tight at every seam and smaller thread than he had ever seen. They brung up a shine to please any man's heart.

Hornbeam was about to get down from The Throne when another man showed up. He had not been at Chickamauga but claimed to have been a supply sergeant with Jackson's brigade. Mr. Foster and Hornbeam at once launched into complaints about supply sergeants, especially when it came to food. "Edible would have been appreciated," said Hornbeam.

"Have you ever tried to feed an army?" said the supply sergeant. "Why, I could get artillery shells by the hundreds. But bread flower? Hardly a pound, and even that infested with weevils." He pulled a flask from his inside pocket. "But there was one ration I had on hand no matter what the black-market price." He unscrewed the cap and held up the bottle. "One hundred and thirty proof." He took a healthy draught. Mr. Foster said he never drank before three but was persuaded to take a sip anyway, "in honor of General Lee, may his fame shine eternal." Hornbeam did not need to be persuaded, drank twice, and remained seated.

Shine waited anxiously for an opportunity to ask Hornbeam to pay. The street was filling up with wagons and pedestrians. A man on a penny farthing rode by waving a flag. Two men in costume chased each other down the street, the one dressed as Johnny Reb beating the other painted in blackface with a Union cap on. A band in the park began tuning up. A drum corps hammered away, the sound reverberating from the store fronts. Women twirling parasols and accompanied by their consorts hurried into the park, looking for seats.

Still Hornbeam had not gotten up, until Mr. Foster suggested the former supply sergeant get his shoes shined, too.

Hornbeam slapped the armrest of The Throne. "Let's draw straws! Short straw pays all three." The bottle went around again. Pedestrians had to walk out into the street to get by the men, who had grown expansive in their guffawing about army life.

Shine finally spoke up. "Gentlemen! Please if you could draw your straws now and settle up. I don't want no trouble with the patrolman."

The men laughed, asserting noisily they would run off the damn patrolman, whoever he was, for they had fought in the war and were there to celebrate General Lee. Yet another man, heavyset and wearing a yellow waistcoat which only accentuated his girth, stopped to see what was going on and was offered the bottle. He declined, then gravely introduced himself as grandson to the patriarch Percival Ordan Terwood. Mr. Terwood conceded that he himself had never been in the war, but that his brother had been killed in Pickett's charge, God rest his soul. Nodding to each man in turn,

 House of Poetry

he spoke of the honor of service, the nobility of sacrifice, and the depth of his gratitude to all the veterans who had fought and died "in their sacred duty to preserve our way of life."

The supply sergeant broke in. "Draw straws with us, Percival, and chance a free shoeshine from the Blackie here." So the men all drew straws, or broken-off toothpicks as it happened. Two of the picks were so nearly even that an argument erupted, good-natured but still in earnest.

Shine pulled his shoebox and tools out of the way of their jostling. He would make no twenty or more dollars today, that was sure. All he wanted now was the two dollars he was owed. He watched people stream into the park. All those shoes and another dollar missed with every pair gone by. Finally, the men settled it out that Mr. Percival had the shortest straw. Still he had to be persuaded to pay, but only after he got his shoeshine. Hornbeam got down from The Throne and Percival took his place. He rolled his pantlegs back, for his shoes were hightops, with clasps. "I want the tongue shined too, mind you."

Shine got out his new tin of black polish, sat down on his box, and went to work. He hurried, which drew a complaint. The tongues were a chore. He had to unlace the boots to get to them and lace them back up to just the right tension to suit this Mr. Percival. Just as he was finishing up, a patrolman came rushing across the street, waving his baton. "You boys are blocking up the sidewalk and creating a disturbance. On this of all days!"

The men clamored their objections, proudly announcing they were veterans and duty bound to be here for General Lee. "We thought to get our shoes shined for the occasion," said Mr. Foster, lifting his trouser leg to exhibit the proof.

"All the same, you can't congregate here," said the patrolman. "As for you," he said, shaking his baton at Shine, "get on out of here."

"But I paid a patrolman five dollars to be here."

"You may have paid *some* patrolman five dollars, but not *this* one." He held out his hand and winked.

"But I have no more five dollars."

"Then scram. Vamoose. *Git!* Or do you not understand the King's English?" Again the patrolman winked, and the men laughed. The supply sergeant handed him the bottle.

"You are a card," said Hornbeam, "for a patrolman."

Shine began to pack up.

The patrolman watched him, hands on hips. Suddenly, he poked Shine in the back with his baton. "Say! Turn around. I say *turn around.*"
Shine stood up and slowly turned around.

"I seen you somewhere," said the patrolman, squinting, as if that would help his powers of recognition. "Free Union!" he burst out, his eyes springing open. "I seen you in Free Union. At the filling station. I was gassing up the Ford." He struck his baton against the flat of his hand and came up closer to Shine. "You was lookin' at *my* daughter sittin' in *my* Ford!"

"No! You got it all wrong, Mr. Patrolman. I don't never go over to Free Union. I don't even know the way there!"

Shine's objections only made the patrolman more certain that he had seen him, and that Shine had not just looked at his daughter but *leered* at her.

Shine had been to Free Union that day. While he stood under a shade tree waiting on his brother who had gone in the store he had seen the patrolman. Seen him gas up the Ford. Seen the woman sitting inside. She even looked back at Shine. But it was not the man's daughter, but Bessie, kitchen maid to the Bolster family. She was near white and handsome, her misfortune.

"We could string him up!" said Hornbeam. "I got the rope in my truck." The other men chimed in, even Mr. Foster. "Sure, let's string up the Blackie!"

Mr. Percival and the supply sergeant got hold of Shine by the arms, gripping him so hard it hurt.

People turned to see what was going on. Shine couldn't bear the shame, even with his life at risk. "Mr. Foster, when have I ever done you wrong? When have I ever been anything but good to you and your family? Vouch for me, can you?"

Mr. Foster looked at the ground.

"Much as I hate to," said the patrolman, "I got to intervene here." He pushed aside Shine's shoebox so he could step into the middle of the group of men. He drew in a breath and seemed to grow larger. "Now, I got no objection to you boys stringing up this Blackie. I ought to be the one leading the posse, for godsake. But I am sworn to uphold the law, and lynching is not allowed inside the town limits. So take your hands off him, you two."

Mr. Percival and the supply sergeant were not ready to let go and had to be told again.

All at once the band in the park struck up with "Dixie."

"We are about to miss the very event we came

for!" exclaimed Percival and hurried heavily across the street. Hornbeam followed, then the supply sergeant.

Mr. Foster looked at the patrolman. "I shall see to it this Negro gets off the street. You can go on, I think."

The patrolman studied Mr. Foster and then faced Shine. "Count yourself lucky. If I ever catch you again around my daughter, I shall skin you alive." He tucked his baton back into his belt and strode off.

Shine shuddered inwardly and watched him go.

"I would not have let them string you up!" said Mr. Foster. "They were only having their fun, after all. You can understand. It *is* a special day."

"I am owed four dollars, Mr. Foster. Two customers, one dollar each, two for Mr. Percival's high tops."

"That may be so," said Mr. Foster, "but I am not responsible!" He turned up his hands.

"But you begun the wager, Mr. Foster. That led to the drawing of straws. Somebody's got to be responsible."

Mr. Foster hemmed and hawed. "Well alright. Hold out your hand."

Shine held out his hand.

"Now close your eyes."

"Why?"

"Do you want your money or don't you?"

It was shameful, but Shine closed his eyes.

"There now," said Mr. Foster, plopping money onto Shine's open palm. "Go buy your honey a dress." Then he walked off across the street, to the unveiling ceremony for the General Robert E. Lee Monument, already grandly underway.

Shine opened his eyes. Quarters. Three of them. All heads. Each showed a busty woman in a swirling robe, with a shield at her shoulder and the word "LIBERTY" in an arc above her head.

Bull

A BITTER TRUTH BURNED IN ME: I, MY FA-
THER'S firstborn son, was absent at his passing. He
died alone! In the moment of his final agony, did he
call out for me? Or was he too dignified for that. How
long did he lie unnoticed, stiffening under the sheet?
Was he just one more cadaver shuttled to the morgue?
Over and over I had promised to visit him--once this
contract was settled, or that project initiated, etc. Then
he was gone. Regret like a cancer grew in me. Often, I
came to tears. One evening, while washing the supper
dishes, I lifted from the soapy water a coffee cup which
had been his. The suds slid away, baring these words:
"*Beauty is truth and truth, beauty.*" Truth was torment to
me, not beauty. "Dad!" I cried aloud.

No sooner had the word left my lips than I grew
weak and dizzy. I collapsed to the floor and blacked out.
What happened next I cannot explain, for I found myself being helped to my feet by strangers. I was in a long
line snaking its way toward a tall, imposing doorway,
the word REGRET chiseled into the lintel. Until that
moment I had been conscious only of my own regret.

After shuffling forward a few steps and then
stopping, I summoned up my nerve and tapped the
shoulder of the man in front of me. "What happens
when we get to the door?"

"You get a TVP," he said, eyeing me with concern. "Temporary Visitation Pass. Then in you go, to meet the one you've suffered over." He pressed a kerchief to his eyes.

I wondered if he also had been a neglectful son.

He stuffed the kerchief back in his pocket. "Practice what you have to say. You won't have long." He turned forward as the line began to move.

I hardly needed to practice, for I had been rehearsing regretful apology to my father for years. Yet I did so with special urgency now, sensing that many other persons were doing likewise, our mingled whispers of regret blending into a drone like the monotonous thrumming of insects on a summer's night. One by one the visitants in front of me were ushered through the dark door by a somber functionary in a rumpled coat and crooked tie. When at last I stood at the front of the line, this functionary, after checking off my name on his clipboard, handed me my TVP. It was well-worn, I saw with surprise, wrinkled, stained, and with a corner torn off.

When I took hold of the pass, the functionary did not let go. "You *may* be invited to stay," he said, leaning close. I caught the scent of mustard on his breath. "Believe me, you *don't* want to be stuck there."

I nodded and he released the pass into my hand. "Now step through."

Facing the chilly darkness which swirled between the doorposts, I balked, felt myself pushed, and fell forward. Tumbling, terrified, I clutched my TVP and my glasses. I was sure I had been tricked and would die. Slowly the darkness waned, I came upright again,

     House of Poetry

my speed slowed, and I glided softly to a stop. Dizzy, I lost my balance and fell onto a sofa. Curtains were half drawn across a broad window. Furniture was oddly familiar: end table with lamp, television on a small table, unlit fireplace, souvenirs from Istanbul on the mantle. I was in our leisure room at home! Except the carpet was a bit brighter than I remembered, the brass samovar better polished, the curtains less wan. Could this be the afterlife? Or an episode from the Twilight Zone?

And there he was! My father, not clothed in heaven's glory, but dressed in his favorite button-down sweater, frayed at the wrists. He was stretched out on his old recliner in front of his considerable library, napping, his mouth open. A folded newspaper lay in his lap.

I stepped quietly to his side and examined his face. With his large eyes, well-molded nose, and full lips, he was still handsome, though the skin was shrunken from his cheeks and his hair was very thin. "Dad!" I whispered, "It's me."

He started awake, his head lifting from the pillow. "William!" he exclaimed, then settled back. "How good of you to come."

I was thrilled and disappointed. Was he happy to see me, or merely acknowledging my presence as a guest? Did he love me, or was I just a duty to him? It was the old quandry. I drew up a chair. He twisted with difficulty to look at me. For years he had suffered from a stiff neck, a stiffness which had so permeated his upper body that he could only bend at the waist. Was this to be his eternal condition after his long life as a faithful Christian? Yet I could not picture him otherwise.

I pulled my chair closer, affection for him welling up in me. "Dad--," I said, summoning courage to speak my agonizing apology. But words were insufficient to bear the weight of the complicated guilt I now felt. I only stuttered.

He didn't seem to notice as he lifted the paper from his lap and folded it open. "The headline today," he said, clearing his throat, "announces that the stock market has declined *precipitously*." He thrust forward one hand and opened his fingers like a trumpet blast. "They *say* we are in for an *arduous* recovery."

His habit of quoting from the newspaper annoyed me growing up, as if my concerns were incidental to the business page. I had never subscribed to a newspaper as a result. Here he was, still at it. Regret in me began to wither, replaced by a familiar irritation. "I doubt there's a stock market here."

He put a finger to his temple. "My *father* worked in the stock market, you know."

Typical, I thought: ignore my objections. Change the subject. "I do know. You've told me before."

"Have I?"

Many times. It was almost the only thing, too. Why had he shared so little, of either his father or his mother? I knew plenty about my mother's parents. We stayed with them for a month every year in August, right up through the summer I graduated from high school. Her father took me for hikes or fishing almost every day. But of my father's father, I knew only that he worked in the stock market and spent his evenings reading the newspaper. Yet Dad pronounced the word *father* with grave emphasis, as though that gentleman was a personage of unusual significance, to myself in particular and humanity in general.

          House of Poetry

Regret was my purpose in being here, yet resentment had intruded! I sought a benign topic. In a garden outside the window a birdfeeder hung in a little tree. A finch clung to the rim, closely watched by a cat crouched by a patch of blooming iris.

"Are you happy here?" I asked.

"*Fairly*. It's rather more urban that I would have hoped." He folded and unfolded his hands as he spoke.

Typical again: first the lukewarm endorsement, then a mild, though fatal, criticism. Too often, growing up, I had been the recipient of his barbed assessments. I grasped for something we both loved. "Tell me again how you got the nickname Bull."

He clapped his hands together. "One day, on the schoolyard, I came to *blows* with a fellow. I was so *animated* in the contest that a *spectator* dubbed me *Bull*, and the name *adhered*." Forgetting his bodily stiffness, Dad turned toward me, delighted. "My mother so *loathed* the *moniker* that finally, whenever a boy came to our door asking, 'can Bull come out and play?' she responded, 'I'm sorry, there's no one here by that name!'"

I sat back, amused as always.

"That was a long time ago, William." He patted a small book which lay upon a tea tray. "Pascal's *Pensees* is a comfort now."

It was a somber moment, just what I needed. "For a long time--," I began.

He broke in on me. Another of his habits I couldn't stand.

"You know, the other day I met John Keats."

I looked at him in astonishment. "The *poet*?"

"Yes!" said my father, grandly opening his hands, as if welcoming Keats to be with us. "He is really *quite* a likeable fellow, though somewhat *wan*."

This was my opportunity. "Shall I recite a sonnet of his for you?

"Certainly!"

I sat upright, took a deep breath, and began. Coming to the final couplet I slowed: "*Then upon the shores of the wide world I stand alone and think/Till love and fame to nothingness do sink.*" I sat back, tingling as always when I recited those lines, and we sat together in reverent silence. Or so I thought.

He frowned. "Keats' reputation *really* rests upon his *odes*, you know."

Inwardly, I fumed. From the time I had been a teenager he had insinuated, in one way or another, that my literary tastes were immature.

"'*Beauty is truth and truth, beauty,*'" he whispered. Visibly tired, he lay back in his recliner. I was afraid he would fall asleep, my TVP would expire, and I would be whisked away, my mission unfulfilled.

I pressed his sleeve. "Dad, please, I have something to say."

He turned toward the window, where a fly buzzed against the glass, before turning back to me.

"I am so sorry!"

"Sorry? For what?"

I felt tears welling in my eyes. "You died alone! And I was not there."

He passed a hand slowly across his forehead as if, it seemed to me, he were drawing a veil over that painful moment of final loneliness and my unforgiveable absence. I wished I could take back my words! Moments before he had been perfectly content. I had spoiled that and piled yet more regret upon myself.

He twisted stiffly toward me. "But William, you *were* there!"

That was impossible. I had been living on the Oregon coast the whole year, mucking about in boats, smoking dope, living in a seedy hotel, actively refuting everything he stood for, which of course I had to justify in long letters to him. I had alluded vaguely to some of my more colorful experiences and once concluded by saying, "I have embraced Lawrencian 'phallic consciousness'!" My father had written back, in his distinctive hand, to say that the "obsessions" of D.H. Lawrence for "sensual pleasure" were "largely discredited" by the "best critics," and were certainly unworthy of me. Could he possibly have forgotten those months of my absence and our heated correspondence?

Yet he was so certain. "You were seated at my bedside when a nurse came in. A *brusque*, big-shouldered woman in a *tiny* cap. She took hold of my foot in her *massive* hands as though I were a *caber* she would *heave*."

I could picture the scene so exactly I suddenly felt as though I were that very moment living it: "You rebuked the poor woman."

"Indeed, I did! 'Who do you think you are,' I said, '*Florence Nightmare?*'"

My father fixed me with an angry look, as if I were that big-shouldered nurse. The thought flashed through me that I *was* like her. She had gotten hold of his foot, and I had gotten hold of his spirit, clinging to it with my regret. The heavy years of this, self-imposed on his behalf, had been useless to myself and a shackle to him.

"The woman clapped her hands to her broad

hips. 'You are the nightmare!' she *proclaimed*, marching from the room like a *centurion*."

My father accused of being a *nightmare*. Oh, that was rich! I laughed. The *Bull* of childhood, it seemed, had revived in him. My father beamed with delight, watching me.

A doubt stilled my laughter. "You said I was present at your *passing*."

"That *was* my passing! The excitement of the moment was too much for my weak heart. Seeing you was my last memory of earthly life."

He swung his feet off the recliner, stood up straight, and walked with an easy grace to the window. He flung the curtains wide, bathing the room in light. "My! What a marvelous afternoon for a *Wordsworthian* ramble." He turned smoothly toward me, without a hint of stiffness in his neck or back. Color appeared in his checks, and his hair glistened. "Will you join me, Willy?"

I rose happily to his invitation, then remembered the functionary's warning. I reached in my pocket, touched the torn corner of the TVP, and felt woozy. My father stretched out his hand toward me, before fading from sight. I woke to find myself collapsed on the kitchen floor. Slowly, I got to my feet. Water was still streaming from the faucet.

I pinned the Temporary Visitation Pass to the small bulletin board above my desk as a memento. It mysteriously dissolved away in a few days, leaving on the cork a faint shadow and the shaft of the pin oddly corroded.

The Rhino in the Garden

EMILY WENT STRAIGHT UP TO HER ROOM after school and flopped on the bed. What a terrible day! Her teacher had reprimanded her for laughing in class. That boy in the library with the awful breath kept pulling her hair. Her friends had abandoned her at recess. She hadn't finished her math assignment. She'd been kept after school for talking in class.

Downstairs, her father, just home from work, collapsed into his lounge chair and began reading the newspaper.

His adled mother shuffled into the room and stopped. She touched her forehead. "What's that animal with the long horn on its nose?"

Mr. Anderson did not look up from his newspaper. He was used to her interruptions. "Rhinoceros."

She beamed. "Of course! Our high school mascot." She shuffled sideways and rhythmically flung out her hands.   "Go Rhinos!" She kept this up right out of the room.

Mr. Anderson paged to the sports section. The Cubs had battled the Los Angeles Dodgers in Wrigley Field, the fearsome Sandy Koufax on the mound. Plucky Fergie Jenkins had matched him, 0-0, going into the seventh.

His mother shuffled back into the room. "Henry? I think there's a rhinoceros in the garden. Eating Margaret's roses. You know how Margaret loves her roses."

Mr. Anderson lowered his paper. "I'll take care of it, mother."

"Such a huge animal," said his mother, nodding her way out of the room, "with such a tiny tail. Seems like a mistake somehow. . . ."

Mr. Anderson raised the paper. In the seventh, the Cubs scored when Ron Santo doubled off the left field wall, driving in one run.

"Dad!" shouted his son Danny, rushing into the room with a skateboard under his arm. "There'saHUG-ERHINOinthebackyardcouldIlikeboardoffthedeckrail andthenlikeifIlaunchitrightskimoffhisbackbonandarc-liketowhereIrichocetoffthetoolshedandpitchdownthe-backfencemyfriendBrad'llvideo. Can I Dad? *Please?*"

Mr. Anderson threw down the paper and got to his feet. "I can't understand a word you're saying, Daniel! Stand *still*, will you please?"

Danny struggled to do as he was told. "I got this great idea, Dad! Skate the deck rail free sail onto the rhino bounce the tool shed crash the fence somersault back onto the deck rail and Brad to video." He rushed out of the room, then returned. "Okay?"

"First of all, there is no *rhinoceros* in the garden. You've let your imagination run away with you again."

"There is!"

"I'll take you to the skateboard park on Satur-day. Now, give me *one minute* of peace and quiet, will you?"

"Like, the ONE thing I want to do in like, YEARS, I CAN'T!" Shoulders slumped, Danny stomped

     House of Poetry

out of the room.

Mr. Anderson sat down with his paper again.

In the top of the ninth, the Dodgers tied the game. Maury Wills bunted to reach first and stole second. A broken bat single scored him. Only a diving stop in shallow right prevented a double.

A scream launched Mr. Anderson out of his recliner. He rushed into the dining room and found his wife Margaret, her hands clapped to her cheeks, staring out the patio door into the back yard. Emily and Daniel were pressed up against the glass on either side of her. A truly enormous animal—a *rhinoceros*--its rough hide glinting dully in the sunlight like old armor, was slowly trampling down the rose bushes and nibbling off the blossoms, one by one. Its curved horn was at least a foot long.

"My grandmother's heirloom roses, the brute!" wailed Margaret. What are you going to do, Henry?"

"Distract it with marshmallows?" ventured Mr. Anderson. "We threw marshmallows to the polar bears at Brookfield Zoo when I was a kid."

"That's horrible!" said Emily. "Marshmallows are full of sugar and chemicals."

"We could beat on pots and pans," said Mr. Anderson.

"Rhinos have very sensitive hearing!" protested Emily.

Mr. Anderson called 911. The dispatcher berated him as a crank caller. "A rhino in your garden? Give us a break! This channel is for genuine emergencies." She hung up.

"Animal control?" he ventured.

Danny waved his arms. "Is that like the dog

catcher? 'Cause, Dad, like, I think the dog catcher no way has a cage big enough for this, like, HUGE rhinoceros."

"Where's Boopsie?" exclaimed Mrs. Anderson, gripping Mr. Anderson's arm and wildly scanning the room. "Oh my God where's Boopsie?"

The family shared a moment of panic as they realized that little Betsy Ann, age nine months, was nowhere to be found. They scattered through the house, calling out her name, searching under beds, behind sofas, in closets.

Emily went back to the patio door. "Boopsie's in the garden!" she called out. "With the rhino!"

Margaret came down from the attic; Mr. Anderson and Danny came pounding up from the basement. Mr. Anderson's mother toddled in from the bathroom.

Boopsie, naked except for diapers, was sitting between the squat, heavy front legs of the rhino. She picked something off the animal's foot and put it in her mouth.

"It's a White Rhino," said Emily, holding up her phone. "See? White Rhinos are placid creatures, unless disturbed of course."

"I don't care what color it is," said Margaret, unplugging the floor lamp, removing the shade and brandishing it like a weapon, "I'm going to rescue my child!"

"I don't think that's such a good idea, Margaret," said Mr. Anderson.

"Out of my way, Harold."

"Mom!" said Emily. "I have a way with animals. And I'm good at sneaking."

"Say Em!" said Danny, bouncing up and down, "maybeyoucouldhandherofftomeandIcouldbalance-

heronmyheadandjumpthroughthecherrytreeandboun-
ceoffthepicnictableandhurdlethedeckrail!"

"No," said Emily.

Danny slumped.

"I'm not letting you go alone," said Mr. Anderson, rolling back his sleeves and retying one shoe.

Mrs. Anderson put down the lamp. "Hurry!"

Emily and her father tiptoed across the deck
and down the stairs. Once in the garden, they bent
double and crept by the fish pond, the day lilies, the
vegetable patch. They were only a few feet away when
Boopsie crawled under the rhino's low-slung belly. Mr.
Anderson inhaled a bug and coughed. The rhino swung
up its great head. Boopsie burbled happily and picked
off another bug. Emily crawled closer.

The animal shifted, snorted, and fixed its
small, black eyes on her. "Who are *you*?" it said, in a
rich baritone.

Emily was too shocked to answer.

The rhino shifted its bulk and took a step towards her, its heavy foot grazing the child's arm.

"Stop!" cried Emily, thrusting out her hand.
"You'll step on my sister! She'll be crushed!"

"Sister?" bellowed the rhino. "You would leave
your little sister *alone* out here?" "Some sister *you* are!"

"See here!" said Mr. Anderson, standing to his
full height. "I'll not have you talking to my daughter
that way!"

"Your daughter? Good God, where are your
parenting skills! *You* would allow *her*—brave soul--to
encounter *me*, while you *huddled* in the flowers?

"I wasn't *huddling*."

The rhino swung its heavy head back and forth.

"Disgraceful! And this other child of yours, a mere *tot*, neglected to *legion* dangers: sunburn, mosquitoes, *cats.*"

"*You're* the danger, for heavens sake!" retorted Mr. Anderson, thrusting out an accusatory finger. "Intruding upon our garden, gobbling my wife's roses."

Please, stop it you two!" said Emily, alarmed. An idea came to her. "Why don't you two stand together and I'll take a picture. You are such a handsome creature, Mr. Rhino."

"I am most certainly not handsome and shouldn't want to be," the rhino grumbled. "But a picture for my scrapbook would be nice."

Emily fiddled with her phone for longer than necessary allowing Boopsie, after stopping to pick off another bug, to crawl casually out from under the rhino's ponderous head. Her father edged as close to the rhino as he dared.

"Smile!" said Emily, clicking the picture with one hand and with the other taking hold of Boopsie by the bib.

Mr. Anderson, Boopsie gurgling happily in his embrace, hurried back to the house where Mrs. Anderson waited with open arms.

The rhino, flicking away flies with his short tail, watched. Emily watched the rhino. She wondered if he lay down to sleep, and if he did, how he got up again. She thought he must be awfully hot inside his thick skin, and carrying around such an enormous head all day long.

"What is a rhinoceros like you doing in our garden, anyway?" she asked.

"Please, it's Bernard. Or 'Bernie,' if you like."

Emily hesitated. "You can't stay here, you know---Bernie."

"I only stopped for lunch."

"Lunch? You stopped to eat my mom's roses for lunch?"

"Please do apologize for me, will you? They were delightful! A diet of grass gets boring eventually."

Emily was so close to Bernie that she could have reached out and touched his horn, which was thick and crusty looking at the bottom, but smooth and shiny at the point. "If you are only stopping for lunch, where are you going?"

"*Las Vegas*! To launch my singing career. I hope to be the next *Engelbert Humperdinck*."

"Who?"

"The great *Torch Singer*. Would you care to hear a sample?"

"I'd love to!" said Emily, seating herself on a large stone.

Bernie, raising his great head and swaying from side to side, began to sing, slowly and with deep feeling:

> *Please believe me, let me go*
> *For I don't love you anymo-re,*
> *Please release me, let me go,*
> *Please release me and let me l-o-v-e again.*

An awkward moment followed. "Well?" said Bernie at last. "You can be honest. I have a thick hide."

Emily toyed with a stem of grass. "At least there aren't any other singing rhinos in Las Vegas."

"I believe that is *damning with faint praise*," said Bernie disdainfully. "What do you really think?"

"I don't think you want to be the next Engelbert

Humperdinck."

"Oh, but I do!"

"I don't mean you should stop singing," said Emily earnestly. "I just mean that you should be yourself when you sing. Don't try to be someone else. Sing about *your* life and what *you* know!"

Bernie stopped swishing his tail. "I could sing the *Blues*. Rhinos are born with the Blues. You'd be blue too, if you spent most of your time munching grass, all by yourself, under the burning sun, on the vast African Savanna."

"You came from the African Savanna? How did you get all the way here?"

"Astral projection."

"Astral projection!"

"It wasn't so hard. Learning English was more difficult."

"I was going to ask you about that."

If a rhino could be said to smile, Bernie smiled. Or at least Emily thought so. More wrinkles accumulated at the corners of his long mouth. "I accessed the *Universal Archives of All Knowledge*," he said matter-of-factly. "Well, not all knowledge. There's nothing in UAAK about Yellow Submarines. I've looked."

Emily drew closer, venturing to touch his massive shoulder. "Bernie!" she whispered fervently, "if you have mastered Astral Projection, and can access the Universal Archives of All Knowledge—you have possibilities much, much bigger than a singing career in Las Vegas!"

"Did you have something in mind?"

Emily lifted her face thoughtfully to the warm sunshine. "Space exploration!" she exclaimed. "The

Secrets of the Pharaohs! Peace on Earth!" She paused. "Why boys are so weird! Oh, Bernie," she said, flinging her arms wide, "think of the possibilities!"

"I did have my heart set on a singing career."

"I don't mean to spoil your dream! I guess I'm dreaming, too."

"I'll have to think about it," said Bernie. "Seek counseling from the Grandmothers and Grandfathers."

"Grandmothers and Grandfathers?"

"Shaggy ancestors from the last ice age. The elders of our race."

"But how will you visit them?" asked Emily. "The last ice age was, I think, about 12,000 years ago!"

"Time travel."

"You can *time travel*, too?"

"Fairly well."

"You are *full* of surprises!"

"Rhinos are often underestimated."

"Will you ever come back to visit me?"

"Someday."

"You promise?"

"By the hair of my chinny-chin-chin. In fact, pluck a whisker as a keepsake."

Emily got hold of a long whisker right in the middle of his stubbly chin with both hands. She tugged and pulled until finally the whisker popped loose. It was stiff as a bristle.

"Ouch!" cried Bernie.

"I'm sorry!" said Emily, rubbing his chin.

Bernie closed his eyes, delighting in her touch. "Well," he said, opening his eyes, "I must be going. You know, I don't even know your name, and we're practically friends."

"My name is Emily. Emily Anderson. And we *are* friends! I will miss you very, very much!"

"The feeling is mutual, Emily Anderson. Good-bye."

And turning slowly around, Bernie trundled off, dissolving into mist as he went, and singing as he dissolved:

Yesterday, all my troubles seemed so far away
Now I need a place to hide away
Oh, I believe in yesterday . . . .

"Bernie!" Emily cried out, holding up her phone "How can I send your picture?"

Bernie didn't stop, so she took one more in desperation: his huge rear end, with its tiny tail. That picture sits on her dresser, and beside it, a special bottle with his chin whisker inside. Bernie has not yet returned, but Emily knows he will. Oh yes, she *knows*!

Thorn

FRANKLIN WAS RESPONSIBLE FOR THE UP-KEEP of Lee Park, especially its centerpiece, the Robert E. Lee Monument. His friend Sonny was responsible for adjacent Jackson Park, so named for its Stonewall Jackson Monument. Franklin and Sonny met for lunch every working day on old man Hopkin's porch across the street from the courthouse. They used to sit on the wooden bench underneath the century-old oak tree, just this side of the jail cell, where it was said Frederick Douglass had once been held. It was a nice spot. But when C. Boscam Slemp got to be Superintendent, he wouldn't allow it, they being Negroes after all.

Franklin usually brought two ham biscuits with an apple to finish, when apples were in season; Sonny favored butter beans and cornbread, which he carried in a tin box and ate with a fork and spoon. They liked to rib each other as they ate.

"What I don't understand about your Stonewall," Franklin said, one hot day in August of 1928, "is how come he's in such an all-fired hurry? He is galloping off to perdition, you know. Where the rest of the Rebel army has already gone, thank God. Except what old men are still left of it."

"Careful! We're old men too, don't forget."

"Who you callin' old?"

They shook their heads in rueful acknowledge-
ment.

"At least my Stonewall is getting somewhere,"
Sonny said, "even if it is perdition. Your General Lee
looks so mournful and his horse going so slow, he shall
be an eternity getting there."

Franklin chewed on his sandwich, while Sonny
spooned up the last of his butter beans. "Just so long as
they don't drag us with 'em," said Franklin.

"Amen to that," said Sonny, closing up his tin
box.

Franklin got out his penknife and scraped at
his fingernails, while Sonny rolled a cigarette.

That was when Superintendent Slemp came
striding down the lawn. "Hey, you two!" he hollered,
tearing off his hat. "Do I pay you to sit?" Reaching the
street he teetered on the curb, elbows thrust out like
bird wings. He was not about to cross over, because
that was where Black Town began.

"We ain't sittin'," said Franklin, getting up. Sonny dusted the corn cake crumbs from his trousers and
got up, too.

Putting his hat back on, the Superintendent
tapped his foot as if keeping time until Franklin and
Sonny had crossed the street. "Have you trimmed up
those roses like I told you?" he demanded of Franklin.
"We got dignitaries coming this evening, remember."

"Yes sir. Headed to it right now."

"Well, damn it, hurry!"

"You do that, Franklin," said Sonny, winking at
him as he turned to go, "you hurry."

When Franklin came around the front of the
courthouse to Lee Park, he saw a tall, slender boy wear-

ing a bill cap and with a haversack over his shoulder, laying a ladder up against the Lee Monument. The boy got his pantleg snared on the rose bushes. When he bent over to get free, a thorn pricked his finger, which he wagged in the air and then stuck in his mouth.

"I don't want these roses damaged," said Franklin when he got up to him. "Set your ladder over here."

"Don't you tell me what to do, old man."

Franklin would never have accepted such a tone from his own son, but this was a white boy and Mr. Clutterback's son.

"Stand still now," said Franklin, putting on his gloves and taking hold of the boy's pantleg with one hand and the rosebush with the other. He was careful to prevent the thorn from being damaged. Never mind that the pantleg was torn.

Once freed, Percy took hold of a bucket of water and clambered up his ladder to the top of the imposing stone pediment. There the bronze sculpture of a somber General Lee, hat in hand and mounted on his faithful Traveler, was depicted as if passing his troops in review for the last time. With acrobatic agility Percy climbed onto Traveller's rump and began washing the back of General Lee with a sponge. When finished with this section he stood up and grasping Lee's head with one hand, swung around to the General's front, and began dousing his bearded face and the front of his uniform.

Franklin was afraid the boy would fall and knew who would get the blame if he did. "Your daddy not doing the work today?" he asked, as the boy spun around, sat down just forward of the saddle horn, and began sponging the animal's mane and head.

"He's doing Stonewall," said Percy. "I wanted to do Stonewall but he said the pediment is too high for me yet."

"You be careful up there."

Monkey-like, Percy swung underneath Traveler's head. Standing on the narrow baseplate, he grasped the bronze reins and began washing the horse's chest and forelegs, then crawled underneath and did its belly and the inside of its back legs.

"You needn't watch," said the boy, as he slid out from that cramped space, and grasping the tail, sponged the horse's rump. "I know what I'm doing."

"I know you do," said Franklin, calculating where best to position himself, should the boy fall. It was eight feet to the ground and straight into the roses. He didn't want his thorns broken on this boy; he wasn't worthy of them. Somebody else was.

Finally, Percy scrambled his way back to the ladder and down to the ground, where he set the now empty bucket with the sponge in it off to one side. Then back up the ladder he went. Pulling a pair of broad white cloths from his haversack, he toweled dry the General and his horse with the same acrobatic agility as before. Before long he was back down on the ground.

"You are pretty good at this," said Franklin. Percy dismissed the remark with a wave of his hand. "Oh, this is nothing!"

"I wouldn't call it nothing. One day, I expect your father will turn the whole business over to you." Once upon a time Franklin had hoped he might turn over a business of some kind to his own son.

Percy got from his haversack a tin of wax, pried the top off, and set the tin in the sun. "Daddy taught me

     House of Poetry

to get the wax warm first," he said. "The brush takes it up good then."

"Your Daddy taught you well," said Franklin. He had tried teaching his own son about pruning flowers, and grounds work generally, but he hadn't been interested.

"I am going be a sculptor one day," said Percy. He extended his arm upwards toward General Lee and Traveller, as if revealing them for the first time. "There will always be a demand for statues of the General."

Franklin pictured himself, aged and stooped, tending roses at the foot of monuments to General Lee lined up all the way to the horizon. Not only he, but his son—well, not his son—but other sons, and then their sons, a servitude down through all the ages to come.

"Plus a demand for statues of Stonewall, of course," continued Percy. "Not to mention Longstreet, hero of Chickamauga. And Jubal Early, defender of the Shenandoah Valley. The daring cavalry commander, Jeb Stuart. A.P. Hill, killed at the third battle of Petersburg. Braxton Bragg, commander of the Army of Tennessee. Noble Pickett, who led the charge at Gettysburg."

Franklin began to feel ill. He tasted bile on his tongue, felt queasy, and was for a moment afraid he might lose his lunch. "You forgot one," he managed to say in a hoarse voice.

The boy stopped speaking and looked down at Franklin, who was bent over, hands on his knees. "What did you say?" he asked.

"I said you forgot one," said Franklin, slowly standing up.

Percy frowned. "Who?"

Franklin looked at the boy, with his blue eyes and freckles. Into the crown of his bill cap was stitched the figure of a snake and over it the words, "Don't Tread on Me."

"Turner," he said. "You forgot Nat Turner."

Percy repeated the name and then shook his head. "Never heard of him."

"You ought to have," said Franklin, drawing a full breath of air and straightening his shoulders.

"Was he a general?"

"Oh, no, he was no general! He was a minister. A minister who became a soldier of the Lord."

"No minister can be a proper soldier."

"He was not interested in being a proper soldier, young man. He had more important business. God's business. He rose up in righteous anger to bring down judgment upon the wicked."

Percy removed his cap and scratched his head. "What was his battle?"

"His battle was elemental, son. He fought for freedom. He fought for justice. He fought to throw off the shackles of oppression!" Franklin raised his fist in the air. "He marched toward freedom and brave souls rushed from all quarters to march with him."

His fist still upraised, Franklin closed his eyes. He as good as saw the slave masters fleeing and then cut down, the houses set on fire, the animals breaking out of their barns, the white women carrying children and fleeing for their lives. He fairly trembled with the terrible exhilaration of it all.

Just then Superintendent Slemp showed up, beating his hat against his leg. "Goddamn it, Franklin! Have you been idle all afternoon?"

     House of Poetry

Franklin turned slowly. "Be careful now, sir."

The Superintendent stopped beating his hat against his leg.

"They's a snake."

"A snake."

"Yes, sir," said Franklin, taking the clippers from his back pocket. "I went to trim up the roses and saw a snake down in there. He put the scare into me."

"Oh for God's sake, you're a grown man."

"Look," said Franklin, pointing with the clippers. "He lays tight against the stone, just there at the dirt. See 'im?"

The Superintendent leaned over to look. "There's no snake in there."

"Oh, but they is! He got his eye right on you. Really bend down sir and take a good look. He's monstrous."

The Superintendent bent down almost double, his head nearly touching the bright roses, reds and whites for the stars and bars. Franklin got in close behind him, the better to point, but lost his balance, he would claim later. He fell upon the Superintendent, who crashed forward into the thorny roses and was cut so badly by them he had to be taken to the hospital. Within the hour, Franklin was fired.

This did not, however, interfere with his having lunch with Sonny the next day on old man Hopkins' porch.

"General Lee is going to miss having somebody to talk to," said Sonny, spooning up his cornbread and butter beans.

"Slemp can talk to him," said Franklin, taking a bite of his second ham biscuit. "Let him bitch to the

General all he wants."

They ate in silence for a few minutes.

"What are you going to do with your time now?" said Sonny.

Franklin put down his ham biscuit and wiped his lips clean with a napkin, as if preparing for a major announcement, which it was. "I'm going into the rose business," he said.

"I would have thought you'd had enough of roses."

"The thorny rose business."

Sonny put down his spoon.

"Rebellion Roses, I mean to call it. Going to see if I can grow a black rose. With extra sharp thorns."

Sonny wiped his lips with his napkin, and then carefully folded it back into his lunch tin.

"It will be called the Nat Turner."

"Uh oh," said Sonny, tugging on Franklin's sleeve. "Look who I see."

Down the lawn strode the Superintendent, slapping his hat against his pantleg. "Do I pay you to sit?" he called out, as he got to the curb.

Sonny shut his lunch tin and stood up. "I ain't sittin'."

"Then get your black ass over here!"

Franklin looked up at Sonny. "I do have an open position in Sales and Marketing."

Sonny sat back down.

The Superintendent continued to beat his hat against his pantleg. He stuck out his elbows like birdwings. He flung curses.

"We create a whole line," said Sonny. "The Denmark Vesey. A sturdy climbing rose, the Harriet

Tubman. An infamous wilting rose with tiny blossoms called 'The Slemp.'"

Franklin laughed. "Roll me a cigarette."

The men smoked.

The Superintendent had ceased to gesticulate. He put his hat back on. It was surprising how small he appeared, in front of the enormous oak tree. Even the courthouse looked small against it.

A Complicated Evening

TWO YEARS AFTER THEIR GRADUATION from the Standopholus Regional Veterinary College, classmates had gathered at Andrea's place for a reunion of sorts. Everything had worked out; even Soren, who had been her man, until he dropped out the last semester, showed up. Afternoon stretched into evening. Candles illuminated genial faces. Andrea brought out chocolate-covered cherries.

"We're freaks!" exclaimed John, taking two. "We went into vet med because we get along better with animals than people."

Hearty laughter.

"Like when my family went on vacation to this dude ranch," said Alex. "I found this ragged pony standing all alone in the woods. I walked right up to him. His mane was full of burrs. I pulled out every last one."

"He let you?" said Dorothy, touching his hand.

"More than that, he nudged me to keep going! So I cleared his tail. Came back the next day with a curry brush and grain from the barn. Before we left I was riding him bareback. I hated to go home! Made up my mind then I was going be a horse doctor."

"For me," said Liz, "it was a cat."

Soren, leaning back in his chair as far as he could, lost his balance and fell in the bougainvillea, cracking the pot. He had trouble getting to his feet.

Andrea set down the pie she had brought out and rushed over to him.

"I'm fine!" he said

Her beloved bougainvillea was not.

"Anyway," resumed Liz, wishing Soren had not been invited to this otherwise grand party, "*Old Tom* had one eye and half an ear missing from all his fighting. Nobody could get close to him—except me. He would roll over on his back, I'd pat his belly, and he would purr like a kitten."

Story after story followed, about a rabbit with no tail, a wounded falcon, a pair of ferrets, a three-legged mutt named Butch. Soren didn't have a story. "I don't get all touchy-feely about critters."

His remark fell like a weight, crushing conversation. From somewhere in the darkness an owl hooted.

John finally spoke up. "What about you, Andrea? What's your story?"

Andrea slowly spun her wineglass. She didn't want to talk about it in front of Soren.

"C'mon, now!"

"It's embarrassing."

Dorothy leaned over and stroked Andrea's arm. "Darling! We're all a little kooky."

Andrea could agree to that. "My story is about me. *I'm* the animal, really. What a miserable animal I was in middle school."

"You too?" said Randolph.

"One day I came home and bawled. Just bawled! Mom came running. She plumped herself down in the sofa and pulled me onto her lap. I was way too big by

     House of Poetry

then, but it was just what I needed. I blubbered about what a klutz I was. How everybody else was good at something but I was terrible at everything.

"'Andy,' Mom said, 'I don't care if you can't kick the ball over the fence like Corky. I don't care if Katy runs the 50-yard dash twice as fast as you do. I don't care if you can't draw unicorns like Jude. I know you will find your gift, sooner or later.'"

"To Moms!" said Randolph, raising a glass. Everybody joined in except Soren.

"That very night, we heard Mrs. Moffett screaming from her front porch. People up and down the block, some in pajamas, came running. We did, too. "There's a beast in my kitchen," she cried, "a *beast!*"

Andrea imitated, provoking laughter. "Then she threw up her hands and collapsed, blocking the door. A bunch of people rushed to help her, and a bunch ran around to the back door. Mr. Murdock, a retired army officer, stood on the steps holding a garden rake. 'Stand back!' he said, in his general's voice. 'I'm goin' in.' Then he kicked open the door."

"I think I've got a tick," said Soren. He held his arm up to the candlelight.

Nearly everyone got up to look.

"Deer tick," said John.

"Why me?" said Soren.

Andrea rushed into the house and came back out with tweezers, disinfectant, and a bandage. Liz performed the operation; Randolph closed. Everybody returned to their seats.

"So Mr. Murdock broke open the door," said John, "then what?"

"He got tangled in his rake and fell down."

Everybody laughed, except Soren, who continued to poke at the red spot on his arm.

"A bundle of fur with a pointed nose and beady eyes scrambled over him and came straight at us. People screeched and pushed to get out of the way. Somebody shouted, 'rabid!' Mrs. Mullins fell and sprained her ankle."

Soren reached across the table for a bottle of wine, which knocked over a candle. Its flame, before dying, scorched the tablecloth. Hot wax dropped onto Dorothy's skirt. "Shit!" she exclaimed, and then apologized. John gave her his penknife to scrape it off. Andrea offered to get stain remover.

"Never mind," said Dorothy. "So what if the skirt was new?" She would have liked to smack Soren.

"With all the screaming and commotion," said Andrea, eager to draw her friends together again, if she could, around her story, "you'd have thought it was the monster Grendel launching out of the house. These were grown-ups, too! In that moment of pandemonium, I stepped into my authentic self. I was a girl of twelve who felt completely calm and rational among terrified adults. I simply got hold of the *beast*—a frightened baby raccoon--by the scruff of the neck and walked home. I named her 'Shammy.'"

"*Her*? How did you know?"

"Feminine intuition," said Dorothy.

"Partly. But I googled and then looked. Sure enough, the vulva was close to the anus."

"A born vet," said John.

"I begged Mom to let me keep Shammy. But she was adamant. So we took her out to *Fairbrook Animal Rescue.* I loved that place, started helping out on Saturdays and worked there every summer in high school. I stopped thinking about whether I was good at anything, and started thinking about where I was needed. Now I'm surrounded by all kinds of strange animals that need me—lizards, bats, parrots, snakes, even a scorpion."

Soren smacked his beer bottle down. "Animals don't *need* you. *Scorpions* don't need you. They're predator arachnids, for god's sake. They kill."

"Jesus, Soren!" said Randolph, slapping the table. "Animals get injured. *Even* scorpions. People love their animals. *So* they come to us for help. If you don't like that, fine. But be *decent* and keep it to yourself."

"*Decent*. Is it *decent* to cage a bird? Keep a lizard in a glass box? A snake in a space so small it can never uncoil?"

"We don't do that!" said Dorothy.

"It's *worse* what you do: prolong the captivity of animals into decrepit old age. Pity the poor cat, blind and deaf, who ought to have been put down years ago, but endures yet another expensive operation, to postpone his owners' brittle grief."

So *now* you have a conscience!" said John. "Christ!"

"I'm honest. Y'all are dishonest."

Andrea had had enough. "You are mean and cruel, Soren." She pointed to the door. "Leave my house. Please!"

"Fine!" Soren said, throwing down his napkin. "Fine." He pushed his chair aside, made his way around the table, and clumped down the deck steps to a stone pathway through a little garden. No one spoke or moved until they heard the side gate squeak open and slam shut.

They thought he had gone. Actually, he had walked down to the end of the street and then back, thinking he might apologize. He'd spoiled the evening, denounced their heart-warming stories of encounters with lovable animals. The thing was, he had his own story, but it wasn't heart-warming. It was horrifying. Not only had he killed the animal, he killed an innocence in himself. He was just fourteen, acting out romantic notions of himself as a sage explorer, a Jim Bridger mountain man, a Natty Bumpo denizen of the wilderness. His wilderness was "the swamp," a scrap of unusable marshland at the end of town. He'd ridden his bike out there in the predawn winter darkness to set traps, real steel traps his grandfather had given him. He was going to catch a fox, that was his idea. A red fox. It was bitterly cold the next morning when he had returned to check his traps. One by one he found them undisturbed. Terribly disappointing. But even before he got to the last one—concealed beneath a narrow animal trail where it passed under the lowest strand of a barbed wire fence--he heard the trap chain jangle. He pulled his cap back and listened again. Yes! A charge of energy coursed through him and he rushed forward. He'd caught his fox! He found a bloody, furred leg, pinched to the bone by the steel jaws. Shock. Horror at what he had done. This was no fox caught in his trap, no predator animal. It was a rabbit, a poor, pitiful rabbit. When he was little, his Mom had gotten him a pet rabbit, *Peter Rabbit* she called him, from the Beatrix Potter books. Here was Peter's wild cousin caught in his trap. How to get the creature out? He was afraid to touch it, lest it bite. An embarrassing fear, unworthy

     House of Poetry

of a true woodsman! He cast around for a stick, a club. Found one, stood over the animal, struck it, again and again. This happened, he knew it had, but the details he had blocked from memory; they were too horrible. When movement ceased, he pressed the trap spring down with his foot. The jaws fell open. He lifted the bloody corpse in the air and flung it into the weeds. He never trapped again. Never told his grandfather either. Nor anyone.

Soren circled back around the house, on the opposite side from the pathway and gate, and stepped carefully to the corner, where he could hear. They were still talking about him.

"Why does he say such things?" said Andrea.

"He's disruptive!" said John, "It's just his nature."

"Something sets him off and then boom!" said Randolph. "Explosion. Everybody burns."

"As if he's the only one with problems," said Dorothy.

Andrea agreed with these judgments. Still, she admitted to herself, he had a point. It was amazing the money people were willing to spend to keep their pets alive. She often wondered if these animals, if asked, would have wanted to go through any of it. She had begun her career animated by a belief that every creature—well, not every creature perhaps--deserved the degree of attentive care people expected for themselves. Raccoons, cats, dogs, horses, scorpions, and all the rest were as much an expression of life as she was.

But after only two years of practice, she found that she was not quite as sensitive about putting down a pet as she had been at first. Would she be able to muster any sympathy at all at the end of her career, or would the whole business have become merely perfunctory? She hoped not. But even the possibility frightened her. Was her humanity even now ebbing?

"Enough!" said Liz, raising her glass. "A toast, if you please!" She waited until everyone had refilled their glasses and raised them toward hers. "To friendship!"

"Hear, hear!"

Drawing Rizelda

HEATHER LIKED TO DRAW. NO, SHE *LOVED* to draw. Until one day in school, while everybody else was studying for a test, Heather started drawing a gypsy,* with rings on her arm, a scarf over her head, and a bewitching smile on her face. Heather wrote a name under the drawing: Rizelda, Queen of the Gypsies.

Hearing the teacher approach, Heather hid her drawing of the gypsy queen under her hand. Immediately, Heather felt as though her palm were being stabbed with thorns.

Once the teacher had passed by, Heather pulled back her hand. There was Rizelda, with the sharp nails of her fingers poised to strike again. The bewitching smile had become an angry scowl. "Vat are you doink? Tryink to keel me?"

Heather coughed, shifted in her seat, even dropped a book as covering noise. Fortunately, the bell rang and everybody left the room, including the teacher. Heather folded the drawing of Rizelda into her blouse pocket in such a way that she could just see out.

Big mistake. Standing in the lunch line, Heather felt a thorny stinging in her chest.

"I vant zup!" Rizelda cried out.

"What?" said an older boy, turning.

"Cabbage zup!"

"Yuk!" said the boy, leaning away from Heather.

Embarassed, Heather broke from the lunch
line, found an empty table, unfolded the paper, and
drew a bowl of cabbage soup, with wavy lines of steam
rising from it.

Rizelda took the bowl of cabbage soup in both
hands and sucked at it noisily. "Zehr gut!" she exclaimed, smacking her lips. "Now make zleeping peelows. Beeuteeful zleeping peelows!"

Heather spent the rest of her lunch period
drawing pillows of various sizes, plumped together. Rizelda curled up and went to sleep, an angelic smile on
her face.

Heather was tempted to leave the drawing of
Rizelda on the table, in hopes a custodian would sweep
it away, but that would have been cruel. So she returned
it to her pocket and headed to history class.

Apparently, Rizelda liked long naps, for she
was quiet the rest of the day. Not until the middle of
supper did Heather begin to feel the pricking of sharpened fingernails. She excused herself from the table to
go to her room, claiming extra homework. Her parents
were naturally pleased.

"What is it?" Heather burst out, after closing
her door and drawing the paper from her pocket

"I haf no frends!" wailed Rizelda.

"So?"

"How can I leef with no frends!"

"I do," admitted Heather.

"Draw!" commanded Rizelda, pointing a crooked finger.

Heather sat down at her study table and began

drawing friends. This required most of the evening and several sheets of paper, as Rizelda was not happy until she was surrounded by friends and admirers and handsome rascals.

Rizelda greeted them all warmly "How are you, my darlink!" "Charmed!" "Oh, you devil, you!"

Heather was having trouble staying awake by the time she had finished with the friends and admirers and handsome devils. She changed into her pajamas and climbed into bed.

Rizelda shook her. "Eef I haf frends!" she exclaimed, "I must haf party!"

Heather yawned.

Rizelda clicked her fingers. "I am vaiting!"

Heather climbed out of bed and went to work. She drew balloons and streamers. Musicians with tambourines. Dancers with belled slippers. Even a suspicious fellow with a wax-tipped mustachio. She spent a lot of time drawing food, mostly desserts. She even drew in a few cats and one greyhound. All of this took many more sheets of paper.

Exhausted, Heather went back to bed. It was hard to sleep for all the merry-making. "Oopah!" cried Rizelda.

If a big mess was any indication, Rizelda's party was a very good time, for in the morning Heather found that her drawings were a terrible jumble of torn streamers, popped balloons, and half-eaten desserts. The partygoers lay sleeping at odd angles on the floor, some of them snoring. The cats were snoozing together among the pillows. The greyhound occupied the couch.

Rizelda, a red scarf tied gaily around her neck, was wide awake.

"Draw Bazaar!" she cried, dragging Rizelda out of bed. "Vegetable zellers! Fortune tellers! Acrobats and animals! Much peoples crowding narrow streets and noisy shops!"

That was a lot to ask, since Heather needed to get dressed, eat breakfast, and catch the school bus.

Rizelda insisted. "Bazaar ez life!"

Heather stopped combing her hair. "Please! Only the fortune teller with her crystal ball. The rest when I get home from school."

She thought it would be a relief being away from Rizelda. It wasn't. She missed her—and her friends and admirers and handsome devils. The school day lagged. She fell asleep in her chair and was sent to the principal's office.

When Heather got home she went to work at once, drawing the busy bazaar, with the vegetable sellers, fortune tellers, narrow streets and tiny shops crowded with people. She even drew in a few stray dogs, two roosters, and a pair of goats. She laid out the drawings side by side.

"Wunderbar!" exclaimed Rizelda. At once she haggled with a vegetable seller, consulted with a fortune teller, and jostled with the peoples in the narrow streets and tiny shops.

Rizelda came out of the bazaar swathed in beautiful scarves and wearing jingling bracelets. "Draw geepsy caravan!" she cried, waving her hand in the air. "Vagons loaded down with spices and ivory from far over mountayns!"

Heather had hardly started when Rizelda gripped her arm. "Now caravan eez suddenly surrounded by bandits," she said in a trembling whisper, "weeth gleaming swords and dark eyes! And I, Rizelda, Queen of the Geepsies eez captured by handsome Bandit Chief!"

Draw!" she cried.

Heather thought about the drawings ahead of her: the gypsy caravan, the distant lands, the bandits with swords and dark eyes, and Rizelda, Queen of the Gypsies, captured by the Bandit Chief. What would Rizelda want her to draw next? This could not go on!

Heather hit on a desperate plan. "I'll draw the gypsy wagon first."

It was a beautiful wagon, carved and painted in bright colors with velvet curtains in the windows, and small bells dangling from the roof.

"Gut! Zehr gut!"

"I'm not sure about the inside," said Heather. "Would you mind taking a look?"

Rizelda, in her scarves and jingling bracelets, climbed up the steps into the gypsy wagon with the velvet curtains, and sat down on the cushioned seat.

"Close the door. See if the latch works."

Rizelda closed the door.

Heather, with a pang of conscience, erased the doorknob, then the door.

"Tr-rickster!" Rizelda cried. "I vill put spell on you for thees!"

Heather did her best to ignore the threat and kept erasing until nothing was left of the gypsy wagon but a gray splotch and eraser crumbs. What a relief! Heather got into her pajamas and went to bed and slept all night without interruption. Her days became ordinary again. Which caused her to wonder about the gypsy caravan to distant lands, the bandits with swords and dark eyes, and Rizelda, the Queen of the Gypsies captured by the handsome Bandit Chief.

Finally one day Heather took out a fresh sheet of paper. Dare she begin? She sharpened her pencil. "Draw!" she said to herself, imitating Rizelda.

Neither Heather nor her narrator understood that Rizelda deserved rightfully to be called "Roma."

Fresh Child of God

"NANSE!" OLD BANETREE CRIED OUT, "HURRY with my Julep." His exclamation was followed by a bout of coughing.

"Yes, Mr. B," Nanse called back from the kitchen, "be right in." The important ingredients were the double shots of bourbon, the sprig of mint, and the tall, dented, tin cup it was served in, a family relic that harkened back to before the war, when the Banetree family operated a plantation that nearly spanned the valley. Concoction complete, she came through the door into the cavernous great room, with its dark, scratched furniture and frayed rugs.

Old Banetree was sunk in a cushioned chair by the fieldstone fireplace, which, this time of year, was cold and dark. He leaned forward just enough to take the offered cup and sucked greedily at the liquor, wetting his untrimmed mustache. With a satisfied smack of his lips, he set it down on a side table, and lay back in his cushioned chair. Once a bellowing ox of a man, old Banetree was now shrunken, his very astringency seeming to be all that kept him alive. His hair, still dark, clung tenaciously to his scalp in a sharp widow's peak. He sat with his legs thrust out, as if resisting the inevitable slide into the grave, and considered the view of his landholdings through the tall front windows.

Nanse sat down nearby on a three-legged stool. She, too, considered the view, and the work to maintain it, especially the boxwood hedge, which needed trimming. That had been her brother Sophocles' duty. He had sworn that one day he would quit the Banetree place and head north for Chicago, which finally he did. That was in 1914, ten years past, and nothing had been heard from him since. Yet the syllables of his destination had remained for her as exotic as those of *Constantinople.*

Old Banetree once again sucked at his drink. "Am I not a patient man?" he said, eyeing Nanse.

"Yes, Mr. B, people say so. Mostly."

"Too goddamn patient! Not like my son, now. He's got fire. He'll need fire to run this place when the time comes."

She dreaded that time. Everybody that sharecropped the Banetree land did. To forestall it, she worked to keep the old man happy and alive. Alive, at least. People counted on her for that.

Old Banetree plucked out the sprig of mint and chewed it. "There is a limit to my patience, Nanse."

"Lord knows, Mr. B. But your people they work hard. They do."

Old Banetree took another drink. "So you say. But I know better. Take the Bottoms bunch."

He called them the Bottoms bunch because they cropped tobacco in the bottom land, by the river. There were three of them: father, mother, and a pretty girl named Ruby. Year after year, the father and mother and now the daughter grew the best tobacco. "I have told them and told them, 'clear that thicket at the river edge.'" He coughed heavily, his face growing red and wiped spittle from his lips. "I troubled myself to ride all the way down there yesterday and have a look. What did I find? Thicket at the river edge. Why is that?"

He asked the question as if she knew the answer. She did know. Asa Bottoms, the mother, had crept up to the big house by darkness one night, hardly able to speak. Nanse had to settle her before she could get out of the poor woman what bothered her so. She and her husband and daughter had set about to clear the thicket when Reginald came driving up in his Ford truck. He came to "inspect" their work, he said, then drove both Asa and her husband Caleb out of the thicket, to inspect Ruby's work alone. He did no inspecting at all, except of her. Ruby was terrified of being with child and had eaten a handful of bitter-tasting medicinals to prevent it and about wretched up her insides. Caleb was so maddened he swore to kill Reginald, then grew fearful of the Klan, should he venture such a crime.

"We in an awful fix, Miss Nanse. If my husband don't end up killed, God save us, or Reginald murdered, or Ruby done to again. . . ." She could not continue.

Nanse had let her speak it all out. Best to just listen and absorb. This she had learned in her thirty-some years as head domestic for the Banetree household going all the way back to Reconstruction days, a household now collapsed to the old man and his violent son. To her the croppers came, seeking remedy for their woes. Who else would care about them? She was their one ally, their only intercessor.

"Please, Miss Nanse," Asa had murmured before going, "is they any way you can help?" The weight of the question, versions of which she had heard plaintively expressed innumerable times over the years, wore on her. She could feel the heavy in her bones.

Nanse was brought back from these reflections by old Banetree's cough. She handed him a kerchief and when he had done coughing handed it back, blood-spotted. "I have half a mind," he said, after his breathing had returned to normal, "to punish those Bottomses with loss of their share for the whole year. Maybe then they will clear that thicket. Or do you have a better idea?" Ever since the second Mrs. Banetree had expired, he had taken to confiding in her.

"They lose their share, Mr. B," she said, "they likely to go hungry. Wouldn't be much good to you then."

"If word gets around they didn't do as they was told and got away with it, why every Negro on the place would think they could do as they please. You know how they are." He finished off his Julep and turned the dented tin cup in his fingers.

"You like another, Mr. B?"

Old Banetree coughed until he was red-faced and then nodded.

"Could be there's copperheads in that thicket," said Nanse, taking the tin cup.

"Could be I guess."

"You don't want your people snake-bit."

"I s'pose."

She let him meditate on copperheads while she made up his second Julep. "Send me down there to find out what's wrong, why don't you," she said, handing it to him.

Old Banetree fixed her with that look of his as he took the drink. She recognized the suspicion in his eyes. He mistrusted her but had to trust her all the same. She could get information from the croppers on his land that he could not. He did not like that, but something was going on down there with the Bottoms family and he must know what it was. Nanse would find out.

"You know I can't have you out of this house."

"Well then, never mind, Mr. B. I don't know what I was thinking."

He raised his hand. "I have made up my mind. You are going."

"Must I?"

"Damn right you must!" he said, slapping the cushioned arm of his chair. "I shall have Toke take you down there in the buggy."

She did not trust Toke. "Oh, don't you waste a buggy ride on me, Mr. B. I can walk."

"Walk! It is three miles."

"That is just the distance I need," she said, standing up and collecting the treasured tin cup, now empty, "to consider how best to speak with that family. So's I can settle the matter. You do want me to settle the matter, I expect."

He pointed a finger at her. "You tell them I am a patient man, but my patience is about at an end, you hear? You tell them if they don't cut down that thicket, I shall drop their share and raise the lease price on their tools. You tell them that."

"Yes, sir."

"Walk!" scoffed old Banetree. "I never could understand the Negro mind."

Because it was already midafternoon and she had not yet given him his foot bath, nor changed his bed sheets, nor made his dinner nor rubbed his back, she decided to wait until the next day before visiting the Bottoms family.

It was a fine morning when she set out. A gentle rain had fallen, cooling the air, and light breezes stirred in the trees. She wore a flowered hat the second Mrs. Banetree had given her. "You deserved better from life," she had said, looking up at Nanse as she lay sweating on her death bed. "Take my hat to remember me by, will you?"

How good it felt to walk! To be just herself, here on this road, walking forward into the world. Out beyond the fields and barns and Negro cabins, the Virginia mountains rose up. She reflected that never in all her sixty years had she been as far as those mountains, nor her mother either, brought here to the Banetree plantation as a girl in shackles some fourteen years before Emancipation. Nanse longed to see what lay beyond those mountains. This morning she felt like she could walk to the ends of the earth.

Her reverie was broken by the roar of an engine. A moment later, Reginald in his dusty Ford truck crested the hill just in front of her. The sight caused her to stop mid-stride and draw in her breath. He had been at Ruby again, no doubt! If only she had come yesterday afternoon, this might have been prevented. The weight of her failure nearly dropped Nanse to her knees. Reginald braked to a stop and leaned out the window, his golden hair gleaming in the sun.

"What's you doing out here, Nanse?"

She turned aside as a cloud of road dust enveloped them, then turned back to him, planting both hands on the truck door, one on either side of his elbow. "Reggie," she said, daring to use his childhood nickname, "what have you done?"

For just an instant, she thought she detected a flicker of admission in his eyes. But that flicker as quickly died with his awkward laugh. "Who are you to reprimand me?"

"You *do* want the tobacco crop tended, don't you?" she said, holding his attention with her eyes.

"Fool woman. Of course!"

"You ain't agoin' to have nobody to farm your tobacco," Nanse said, reverting to the vernacular as she would if anger stirred her deep enough, "if you do to your people what you done to that girl."

He drew back from her a little, enough for her to wonder what had become of the little boy he once had been. He had brought a little bird to her one time, cradling the poor creature in his soft hands, desperate to know if she could fix its broken wing. Now he was a man, broad-shouldered and fearsome.

"It's no business of yours how I manage this farm." He toyed with his truck's gearshift and then revved the engine. "Get on home now."

"Your father sent me."

Reginald glared. "I will soon give the orders here." He sped away, his truck tires kicking up stones and dirt clods against her.

Waiting until he and his Ford had disappeared around a bend, Nanse lifted her skirts and hurried down the hill. Tobacco plants, with their broad leaves, stood up tall and strong in neat rows with the furrows between them clean of weeds. But the Bottoms family was not at work in their field, as they ought to have been. She heard Ruby's screams before she even came in sight of their small cabin under a walnut tree and wished she could tear off her skirts to run faster. She burst open the door and fairly jumped inside. Ruby was curled onto the only chair, sobbing. Her mother, Asa, bent over her. Caleb paced the room, cursing.

Face streaked with tears, Ruby looked up from her mother's embrace. "I can't stay here no more, Miss Nance. I can't!"

"Oh now, don't talk so," said her mother.

"I mean to go!" said the girl, wiping her tears. "Ain't nobody going to stop me."

Ruby's mother turned to Nanse, imploring her help.

The girl's truth was keen. It cut Nanse, too. She didn't want to go back up to the big house for even one more day and tend old Banetree, with his hacking cough and double whiskeys. She was done making peace on his behalf. Reginald would have his way, no matter what she said or did. She reached out her hand to Ruby. "Lead me to the river, will you?"

"You wouldn't dare, would you?" said Asa.

Caleb pushed by her, gripping a knife. Asa followed. What else could she do?

The river on the near side was shallow, with a pebbly bottom. It flowed around a jumble of rocks midway across; most of the current flowed along the far bank, where a pair of sycamore trees leaned far over, half their roots exposed. Nanse bent over and began unlacing her shoes. Ruby, beside her, did the same.

"You don't mean to cross, do you?" Asa asked.

Nanse pulled off her shoes one at a time, tied the laces together, and stood up. "I mean to let these waters wash every trace of Banetree from my soul and step out on the other side a fresh child of God, even at my age." It thrilled her to say those words. She waded out, shin deep. Conscience halted her. Would she leave behind all the other sharecropping families working Banetree lands who counted on her to intercede on their behalf? They would have nobody if she were gone. Nobody. But what of her own self? Did she not also deserve escape while the living breath still rose and fell within her?

Ruby stepped into the river. The muddy current swirled around her feet. Asa and Caleb stood watching from the shore.

Nanse stepped in after her. She turned back toward Asa. "You coming?"

"Yes, Miss Nance," said Asa, "I coming." She put one foot in the water, drew it out again, and looked back at her husband, who stood alone, unmoving, except for turning the kitchen knife over and over in his hand.

"C'mon now, husband."

"Naw! I ain't."

"Daddy? What you mean you ain't comin'?"

"You hear that? Listen to your daughter. Let it go! Just come on."

Caleb turned the knife blade up and felt along the edge with his thumb. "Tell me where you going, and when I have done I will meet you there."

Asa and Ruby looked to Nanse for the answer. She looked down at the muddy water making soft ringlets around her legs, then to the far side. She waded back to shore and went up to Caleb. "Give me the knife."

He shook his head.

"I'll take care of it. Give me the knife."

A heron glided by and settled itself downstream on the far shore, bent slowly forward and stiffened, waiting for prey.

"If you mean to end your troubles with it, you are wrong."

The heron pierced the water with its long beak like a spear and brought up a wriggling fish. Pointing its beak in the air, the bird adjusted the fish face forward and then swallowed it. Down the long, slender neck went the lumpen fish toward the elastic stomach with its stew of digestive acids.

"Your wife and daughter need you. Give it a-me."

"Where you going to?" said Caleb.

"Chicago," said Nanse, enjoying the musical syllables. "The city of Chicago."

Caleb felt of the knife edge again and backed away from her. "Goddamn son of a bitch."

The heron lifted slowly into the air and flapped its way soundlessly downriver.

Nanse sighed, nodded, and returned to the river. She joined hands with Asa and Ruby and they waded out together. The going was easy until they got near the far shore, where the current ran. They let go of one another and swam, but got carried downstream, until Asa caught hold of a tree root and Nanse caught hold of her. Ruby's head went underwater, but Nanse thank goodness managed to catch hold of her hand. They drug themselves up onto the bank and sat dripping in the tall grass. Caleb was gone. Ruby began to cry.

Nanse caught hold of her hand and stood up. "Come now, child, we got a far distance to go. Your daddy he coming later on."

Asa got to her feet, too. Together, dripping wet,

the three of them walked the dusty road. The sun was warm and good. Nanse was happy at first to be going. But Caleb and his knife weighed on her mind. Nothing but trouble would come of his violence. He might die from it, as well as Reginald. But other families would be left to live the consequences. The Smith family, with their soft-headed boy. The widow Tansy. The Sublets, with their dozen children and how many cousins. Others. No, it wouldn't do to run off like this. She stopped walking.

"What's wrong?" said Asa.

"I must go back."

Ruby took her hand, begged her not to.

Nanse shook her head. "I'm sorry."

Asa pulled Ruby to her. "Look after my Caleb, will you?"

"I will." Nanse reached into her sweater pocket. "Open your hand."

Asa had been swatted across her hand many times as a child. The sting was a permanent, searing memory. "Why?"

"Please. Just do."

Asa slowly complied.

Nanse laid a wet, folded wad of bills in Asa's trembling hand and laid her own hand over it.

"When you get settled, send me a letter, you hear? Now take Ruby and go on. Go on to *Chicago*."

Worry Thee Not, Friend Parker

DAN'L BOONE AND ME HAD JUST SET IN FOR the long trek home to Yadkin County, North Carolina. We was well-pleased with our expedition, both horses loaded heavy with furs—beaver, mink, fisher, otter. Even had two buffalo hides we'd traded for. We was hikin' up this mountain trail, leadin' the horses careful on foot, Dan'l in front with the paint, me behind with the bay. Come around a bend to find a nice turn-out, all shaded, with a cold spring, stones set around to pool the water. An Indian way station, sure enough, with sign everywhere warriors been there that very morning. I was jumpy and eager to quit the place, soon as we had watered the horses.

But Dan'l he set down and leant easy aginst a big oak. He begun to nod.

"Dan'l!" I says, "We got to go."

Dan'l he opened one eye. "Worry thee not, friend Parker," he says. "The Native will not kill a sleeping man. His honor forbids it."

"Maybe so," I says, "but that don't stop him from torture!"

Dan'l he just waved off my words like so many skeeters. I set guard, and with a thumb on the hammer of my flintlock. But I was trail-tired, and damn if I didn't fall asleep, too! Woke to myself grabbed by the arms and jerked to my feet. Dan'l besides. The two of us poked and prodded by Shawnee warriors, some with guns, some with bows. Then their chief steps through. All plucked and painted he was, an' feathered like a turkey gobbler in strut and got a longknife in his belt. I thought sure we was dead men.

He thumped his chest and says, "So, the great Boone!"

Dan'l thumped his chest and returned the compliment: "The great Chief Blackfish!"

My God, I thought, it's *Bloody Blackfish* as caught us.

"We take horses," he says. "You go home, Boone," Then away the whole band went, with our horses in tow.

Dan'l he don't pay no mind, jest set off hikin' back down the way we had come.

"What of our provisions?" I says, tryin' to keep up. Dan'l he set the devil of a pace. "We ain't got a bedroll, nor a crust of bread, nor a thimble-full of whiskey!"

"Worry thee not, friend Parker," he says. "We shall get our horses back." Then he spranged into the woods, quick as a mountain cat.

I waren't near so quick, being more possum by nature, so's I had a deal of trouble followin'. After much slow and tedious trackin,' for Dan'l he could speed through the woods without leavin' narry a leaf out of place, I found him, still as a fawn, nestled down beside a tree. Just before sunset, here come Chief Blackfish and his band, with our horses in tow, there on a trail below us.

"Moan," says Dan'l, leanin' close, "moan as if

mournful death itself were upon thee."

"That don't seem like a very good omen," I whispers back.

"Worry thee not, friend Parker," says Dan'l, "just moan." Then he slunk down toward the Indian camp through the moony woods.

So's I commence to moan, as told. Never until that very moment did I know I was such a moaner, natural-born! Moan low, and moan high, moan like the souls that was damned to perdition, moan like the witches a-flight in the skies, moan like the awfulest, drawed-out, painfulest death that ever was died by any man that ever was. Why, I got so full of the moaning spirit that I begun to throw in a cough or two, and then I got to sputterin' an' retchin' an' a deal a throat-rattlin', an' overall the right woefulest sounds of death and dying you ever could imagine.

I never knowed moanin' was such a hard business though, for my lungs got about moaned out, and my head dizzied. I thought what a sorry thing it would be if in the midst of all this moanin' I myself should expire from it! Right then I was grabbed up *agin* from behind by them self-same Shawnee that had grabbed me up before. Chief Blackfish he clapped his hand over my mouth so hard I like to suffocate. I was damn sure I was a dead man, this time, with first my fingernails turned back and then my scalp took.

But no! For there was cries of "Boone! Boone!" and down yonder somewhere the sound of hoofbeats!

Chief Blackfish he unclapped my mouth and shoved me to the ground, and off at a run went the whole bunch.

"Jumpin' Jehosophat!" I shouts, enjoyin' the tug

of hair still on my head, "the great D. Boone has done out-foxed 'em! All on account of my *moanin'*. Outstandin', Parker Fitzpatrick, outstandin'!" Realizin' my dismal situation I sobered up, being *lost*, Dan'l gone with the horses, and Chief Blackfish with his warriors mad as hornets.

Then come a hand on my shoulder. I was plumb *positive* I was a dead man, with first my eyelids cut off, before my nails was turned back and my bloody scalp took. But no! For it was Dan'l. His very own self, with the horses beside, both the paint and the bay. "Worry thee not, friend Parker," he says.

I was full to burstin' to know how he'd managed to steal back our horses, and so easy in the adventure besides, but kept quiet, fell in behind him, and away we went at a stiff pace all night and on into the next day, with no more mischief from Chief Blackfish and his band.

Or so I thought.

For near evenin', with Dan'l still pushin' on at a steady dog-trot and me hankerin' for vittles and a draught of liquor, we passed under a leaned-over tree which in my starved condition bore a strikin' resemblance to sausage. Down from the branches of that tree dropped the *same* Shawnee warriors as before. Out from behind a boulder stepped ol' Chief Blackfish, with his eye upon me and longknife raised up. I thought for *damn* sure I was a dead man then, after my nose was cut off, my eyelashes sliced away, and my bloody scalp took.

But no! The chief sheathed his knife and turned to Dan'l. "So! The great Boone. Again."

Dan'l touched his hat. "The great Chief Blackfish. Again."

"Clever Boone."

"Not so clever as thee."

The Chief he just barely crack a smile. "We take horses second time. No more. So the great Boone he come with us. All go to home country. Make Boone *Shawnee*."

"Be glad to go," says Dan'l. "And live as Shawnee, too."

No way did I want to go, 'specially in company with the Chief and his armed warriors. But if Dan'l would go, then so would I. We was partners. Only that was not what Chief Blackfish had in mind. He pointed at me with that damned knife of his and says, "noisy night devil he not go."

Noisy night devil. Huh! Once I got over the insult I begun to worry. Just how was I to get back home? No horse, no provisions, no powder nor shot 'cept what I had on me, and no whiskey. Going all alone through Indian country. I didn't like my chances, not a'tall. Worse of all, Dan'l, my partner through many an ordeal and adventure, seemed to have give me up altogether. That was mighty hurtful. I stood mournful by a tree as Chief Blackfish and his band turned to to go, with our horses in tow and Dan'l in good humor with 'em!

"One problem, Chief," he says.

Chief Blackfish turned. "What problem?"

"The noisy night devil here. He shall follow along behind us, moaning as he goes."

Chief Blackfish scowled. "I cut off his lips. He no moan then."

I clapped my hands over my mouth. "My God," I thinks, "no more talkin' & no more kissin'!"

Dan'l he shook his head. "You could," he says. "But then he'd wail. Which would be worse."

"I *kill* him," says the Chief. "He no wail then."

Dan'l shrugged. "If you must."

I shuddered from top to bottom. Would Dan'l give me up so easy to death? And disemboweled first, no doubt!

Two warriors got hold of me, so tight about the arms I thought my bones would break.

"You might," says Dan'l. "But then he would be a spirit, and never would his moanin' cease. *Never*."

The chief eyed Dan'l. He motioned the warriors to let go a me and step away. I could have crowed like a rooster just then, if I'd dared.

"Clever Boone," says the Chief. He stood silent a good long while. Finally, he sheathed that god-awful knife. "Take noisy night devil back to your country."

"Horses, too?" says Dan'l.

The Chief nodded.

No more questions asked, we took holt of our horses and struck out home to Yadkin. I kept turnin' back, to see if them Shawnee was followin.

"Worry thee not, friend Parker," says Dan'l, "Worry thee not."

     House of Poetry

The Celebrated Humorist

THE CELEBRATED HUMORIST HAD BEEN years on the circuit. He would have long since quit the business but for his failed real estate speculation. Worse by far, his only daughter was stricken with tuberculosis. He had found a sanitarium for her, but it was expensive. So he had cobbled together this one last tour.

As it had been in every city he visited, the auditorium that evening was packed. People had waited hours for tickets. Nothing could be worse than pushing a crowd past its patience; certain belligerent patrons had begun whistling and stamping their feet. Yet the celebrated humorist remained seated behind the stage curtain, massaging his feet and sipping a whiskey. He was thinking back to his unlikely beginning in this unforgiving business.

One day in school, he had snuck off the playground during recess, with no purpose except to escape kickball and jump rope. After pushing through a cordon of bushes he noticed a break in the fence which bounded school property. Squeezing through, he discovered a little stream, which he followed with all the zeal of a renowned explorer. Inching down to a sparkling pool, he lost his footing and slid into the water. A shard of rock cut his ankle, right through the sock, drawing blood. Clambering back up to the pond rim he examined the shard and realized it was an arrowhead, nearly complete, about three inches long, neatly made, its edges knife-sharp. He wondered how many hundreds of years it had lain there, and what skillful hand had shaped it. These delightful ruminations were sharply interrupted by the distant sound of the end-of-recess bell. Clutching the arrowhead, he rushed back to the schoolyard. Old Hickens caught him by the shirt-collar and marched him to the principal's office.

"Why are your pants all wet, Henry?" the principal demanded.

Henry opened his hand to reveal the gleaming arrowhead.

"Where in heaven's name did you find this?"

Haltingly, Henry described his expedition, fearing punishment.

"You may have saved our school, young man!"

Henry was astonished to hear this. "From what, an Indian attack?"

The principal earnestly explained that his discovery of an arrowhead required that state archaeologists exhaustively examine the site, which meant that further planning for an interstate highway would be suspended until the examination was completed, which could take months. Should archaeologists discover evidence of an Indian village, especially one with a burial ground, the highway might have to be re-routed altogether and the school spared from demolition. Never before had an adult shared such weighty information with Henry.

On the school bus the next morning, he saw the driver's newspaper lying open: *Small Boy Discovers*

    House of Poetry

Ancient Arrowhead. He wasn't *that* small, he thought. Besides what did smallness have to do with his discovery? His sudden notoriety drew mockery from the school bully. "Where's your bow and arrow, Injun?" he taunted, performing a mock war dance. However, Marybeth Daltry, with her gorgeous hair, took such pity on him she invited him to eat lunch with her in the cafeteria. To be so near to her overwhelmed Henry's senses and he could barely finish half his sandwich. He reveled in her earnest questions about his exploit. "I might have drowned," he said, a remark which elicited such a look of admiration from Marybeth that Henry dared not take it back.

The celebrated humorist sipped his whiskey and smiled at these memories. Such trouble he and that arrowhead provoked! Artifact hunters from out of town showed up and began digging holes everywhere, not just around the beautiful pool, but on the schoolyard, including where kickball was played. *No Trespassing* signs were tacked up: *Violators will be prosecuted to the full extent of the law.* Altercations ensued. Angry citizens gathered on the playground waving placards, for or against the highway, in favor of a new school building, opposing more taxes, demanding protection of tribal lands, lobbying for a Walmart. The mayor called a town meeting, which turned to argument. Tempers flared. Men raised their fists. Women swatted each other with their purses.

The celebrated humorist chuckled. His boyhood self had gotten so fed up with the adolescent behavior of these adults that he had climbed on a table and shouted, "Stop!" Everybody in the room got quiet. He held up the arrowhead. "The Indian who shot this," he exclaimed, "might have missed his deer, but he sure stirred up a hornet's nest!"

Everybody laughed and applauded and were civil towards each other again. Henry knew right then and there he could command an audience. On that confidence, he had built a career.

In all the years since, he had never provoked more hearty laughter nor produced a more salutary result. He pulled a kerchief from his pocket and daubed at his eyes. He had become too *studied* in his performances over the years, too *practiced*, less *honest* in drawing a laugh from his audience.

He tucked the kerchief back in his pocket, and took a last swig of whiskey. The crowd was stamping in unison, like a mighty army coming for him. He slipped his shoes back on, straightened his bow tie, rolled his shoulders, took a deep breath, and came around the curtain. Thunderous applause greeted him. He relished the moment, as he always had, stepped to the podium, and put on the wry smile for which he was so well known. Once the applause had subsided, he took hold of his right earlobe and tugged, pretending to wince. It was a signal the crowd understood. The stooge got to his feet, dressed in baggy clothes and holding a crushed hat. "Were you born funny, sir?" he called out.

"Gosh sakes, no," said the celebrated humorist. "I was born sour."

A ripple of laughter spread through the audience.

"I was the last of twelve children. My mother, bless her soul, was exhausted from child-rearing by then. I was obliged to change my own diapers, amongst other ignoble tasks of infancy."

          House of Poetry

Another ripple.

The stooge scratched the back of his head. "Did you attend school?"

"I did," said the celebrated humorist, stroking his beard. "Mostly sitting in the principal's office. I suppose this was meant to cure me of mischief."

More laughter, sustained this time.

"Then how did you get so funny?" asked the stooge, twirling his crushed hat.

"By accident."

"Was it severe?"

"Not severe enough. I survived. Much to the chagrin of my detractors."

The laughter was general by then, punctuated with applause, but the sound meant little to the celebrated humorist. In fact, to a certain degree, he resented it; he could say almost anything, it seemed, and elicit laughter. It was about all people expected from him. *What if I were to simply walk off the stage and out of the auditorium?* That would be a surprise. That would render his audience silent, for a change.

Or maybe not. Because he was silent for no more than two or three breaths before people began shifting in their seats, turning to one another, whispering. What was going on with the celebrated humorist?

The stooge, sensing a crisis, stood up on his chair, and with a dramatic flourish energetically flung his crushed hat into the air. The crowd grew silent, watching the hat sail into the darkness of the vaulted roof. The celebrated humorist watched, too. He would throw his hat into the air just that way when his beloved daughter was a little girl. She would screech and run after it, and he would gather her up in his arms as she, laughing, struggled to put it back on his head and he vainly attempted to resist. He smiled to himself, remembering. How many times had they repeated this pantomime? Now, lovely girl, she was confined to a sanitarium, struggling to breathe and coughing up blood. He was arrested by a consciousness of his own selfishness. What after all was so very objectionable about his present circumstances? So what if he spent his days traveling in cramped coaches, his evenings entertaining strangers in bleak auditoriums, his nights in rundown hotels to save money? If by these inconveniences he could raise the money to sustain his daughter's care--and with luck pay down his debts - he was profoundly willing to do so.

The hat plummeted noiselessly into the orchestra pit. The stooge clambered in after it, but for a long minute did not reappear. At last he climbed back out, punched the hat back into shape and put it on.

"I thought you'd gone to sleep down there," said the celebrated humorist.

The stooge frowned and vigorously shook his head.

The audience tittered, glad to be amused again.

"What took you so long?"

The stooge tapped his chin as if thinking, then lifted his hat to reveal a rabbit sitting quietly on his head.

Laughter and scattered clapping spread through the auditorium.

"Does that creature play an instrument?" asked the celebrated humorist.

The stooge, with clownish exaggeration, shrugged, lifting both hands, palms up.

     House of Poetry

"You got him from the orchestra pit. He must play something!"

"Tuba!" someone shouted.

"Kettle drum!" cried another.

"Pipe organ would be my bet," said the celebrated humorist.

More laughter.

"It's a long shot, I know. But long shots make the big money. Like the hotel I bought. Got it for a song. And no wonder. Somebody'd stripped out all the plumbing pipe. Or the mineral springs I traded for. Turned out the mineral was salt peter. You ever tried soaking in salt peter? Don't."

These confessions elicited mock groans and puzzled laughter.

"Yes, I've spent my money unwisely, but garnered a rich fund of experience, which can't be banked, however. So I save every penny I can--when I have a penny. I don't waste a nickel on haircuts, as you can probably tell."

The celebrated humorist took a slow drink of water, waiting for the audience to settle down.

He turned to the stooge. "I think you can put that rabbit back in the orchestra pit. I believe there's a concert in here tomorrow. He'll need to practice."

This remark drew forth more laughter.

The stooge smiled, lifted the rabbit carefully off his head, cradled it to his chest, and climbed down into the orchestra pit again.

"If he comes back out with a giraffe in tow, or an elephant, I am leaving the stage. You will have to carry on without me. Music or no music."

The laughter was continuous by now. The

evening would be a success. The celebrated humorist could count on a good crowd at his next stop, too. But he couldn't wait to close this evening, and get to the telegraph office, if it was still open, and send a message to his daughter. He hated to think of her suffering, feared that she might pass away while he was on the road. "Please stay alive!" he whispered to himself. "Two months, and I will be at your side."

I Choose Elegy

DAVID RAISED HIS HEAD FROM THE PILLOW when I opened the door.

"Well," he said, laying his head back down with a sigh, "you're here."

I liked visiting him late at night, in his simple room. The preoccupations of my daylight hours evaporated in his presence. I pulled up a chair and sat close.

He was feeling a little better this evening. Two young ladies had visited him in the morning, for physical therapy and to give him a bath. "They were so bright and enthusiastic. It was wonderful!" He raised his bony hands and clapped.

The sight of his thin arms and mottled skin troubled me.

"They asked, 'what did you *do*?' When I told them 'I was a professional dancer in New York City,' their eyes got so wide!" He laughed, and behind his thick glasses mimicked their expression. "'I'm in the poster,' I told them."

I had looked at this poster on the opposite wall every time I visited. Ballet dancers, red as the setting sun, had leapt into the air, where they would remain forever poised, like figures on Keat's Grecian urn.

"I'm in front."

I walked around his bed to get a better look. I wouldn't have been able to tell it was David. The young man was so beautiful and muscular. His back was arched and his left arm and hand were extended in a graceful curve, as though he were lightly embracing a spirit. His expression was rapturous.

I came back around his bed and sat down. I looked at the poster again. Unreadable script scrolled along the bottom and up one side.

"Tokyo," he said. "We were doing a Bach piece, the last movement of the Brandenburg Concerto." He hummed a few notes, with sprightly verve. "It was Doris' last piece."

Doris Humphrey and Charles Weidman were part of the Denishawn School of Dance, along with Martha Graham. They broke off to form their own dance company. This as David had taught me was the lineage of Modern Dance, and he had been a participant, dancing for Doris and Charles, and later for Jose Limon.

"It was an incomplete piece," he said. "Doris wasn't well."

We were silent together.

"Would you like me to read a poem?" I asked.

"I'd love it! Which one?"

I suggested *Ode to a Nightingale* or *Elegy, Written in a Country Churchyard*, and at once was keenly embarrassed that I had offered to him poetical musings on death when in his hours alone he must have been meditating on its imminent approach.

"I choose *Elegy*."

While still paging my way to the poem, he began to recite: "*The plowman homeward plods his weary*

     House of Poetry

way, / And leaves the world to darkness and to me.'"

He closed his eyes and waited.

I leaned toward the small light on his night table and picked up where he left off: "*Now fades the glimmering landscape on the sight, /And all the air a solemn stillness holds.*" The stillness felt even more solemn because the old volume from which I read, with its cover half gone, was filled with my father's marginal teaching notes. I finished and closed the book.

David was not finished. He opened his eyes: "'*Full many a flower is born to blush unseen, / And waste its sweetness on the desert air.*'"

He was that flower, almost. The desert was his poor childhood and dominating father in rural Georgia. Yet he did blush in time, well seen, too, a miracle he himself could hardly comprehend.

"My grandmother had a picture on her wall," he said, "of a little black boy in bed between two huge white pillows, with the covers pulled up under his chin. Under the picture were the words: '*far from the madding crowd.*' I loved that phrase, though I never knew until years later where it came from!"

He fairly warbled with laughter, and I laughed, too.

"She lived in Miami and hosted a family reunion when I was ten. Her house had a second floor, where I looked out the window. Such a view. *Poinsettia* and a *papaya* in the front yard. *Lovely*!"

His love of flowers was ardent to the point of theft. I took him on a garden tour once and he kept pinching off sprigs of blooming plants to take home. I was fearful we would be rebuked but he was cheerfully cavalier.

"Such a beautiful poem," he murmured.

I wished that I could speak a single line as beautiful and transfigure this simple evening into art as David's spirit ebbed away before my eyes. The best I could think to do was lean over, touch his forehead with my kiss, and go.

A Burst of Sunlight

EVERY MORNING AT DAYLIGHT SETH JOHN-SON walked out to the curb and got the paper. This morning the paper was not there. Not on the sidewalk, not hidden in the day lilies by the mailbox, not in the street. Then he remembered why: it was Easter. He felt a gust of warm air and saw his neighbor's yard full of robins. Spring! Nature returning to life. That was the true resurrection. A wonderful idea sprang up in him: a Sunday drive up on the Blue Ridge Parkway, with a picnic at a scenic overlook.

Rushing back in the house to share this idea with his wife, he found her, still in her bathrobe, making coffee. Seth admired her still graceful form. Fifteen years they had made home together, raising three children. Even during his shaky business ventures, she had remained affectionate and supportive. Brimming with gratitude, he slipped behind her and pressed his body against hers. She shrieked and dropped her coffee mug. Hot coffee went everywhere. Seth dropped his arms and stepped away.

Sybil turned on him. "Don't scare me like that. I've told you!"

She had, many times. How could he forget? He apologized, as usual. She cleaned up the spilt coffee, took down his favorite mug and offered him a cup fresh from the pot, with cream.

Seth declined, a penance.

"Take it!"

He hesitated, long enough to verify his remorse, and gratefully accepted the coffee mug from her. He inhaled the aroma of the hot brew, sprinkled with cinnamon. "How about we take the kids for a drive up on the Blue Ridge Parkway and have a picnic?"

"When?"

"Today! After breakfast."

Sybil put her coffee down. "Did you look at the calendar?"

Seth shook his head.

She led him by the sleeve to look at it, posted on the wall above the fruit basket, and pointed out that she had a yoga class at 11:00 and a book club at 3:00. "Why do you spring these ideas on me at the last moment?"

"What's wrong with a little spontaneity, now and then?"

"Nothing! But you expect me to just drop everything any old time you've suddenly got an 'idea.' You could plan a little. Take *my* life into account, now and then."

Seth stood immobile, weathering her rebuke.

Jason, their oldest at fifteen, shuffled into the kitchen, hair awry and a skateboard under his arm.

"Do you sleep with that thing?" asked Seth.

Jason put the skateboard on the floor, stood on it, and reached into the cabinet for the Cheerios. "It's not a *thing*, Dad, it's my *transportation*." He coasted smoothly out of the kitchen and into the dining room, nibbling from the box as he went.

Seth felt like grabbing the box from his hand and stomping on it. A terrible thought. How quickly his joyful idea of an Easter outing with his family had deteriorated into squabbles. Fine. He opened the door to the basement.

Sybil watched him. "Are you leaving?"

"Going down to my workshop."

"Now? I thought you wanted to go for a drive on the Parkway.

Seth shrugged.

"I'm making blueberry pancakes."

His favorite. Nursing his injured pride, he went down in the basement anyway.

"What's wrong with Dad?" he heard Remy, their youngest, ask, as he closed the door behind him. Ayla, age thirteen, was talking to somebody on her phone. Skipper barked. Seth turned on the light and sat on the wobbly stool in front of his old workbench crowded with various projects half completed and knick-knacks needing repair. He clicked on the small heater at his feet, picked up a screwdriver and put it back down. He wished he'd not come down here. But it would be silly to tromp back upstairs right away. So he remained obstinately seated, glumly fiddling with the pieces of a painted ceramic face which had fallen off the dining room wall. The neighbor's damn cat appeared in the little window above Seth's tool shelves, starring down at him as if he were a museum exhibit. That was too much. He turned off the light and heater and went back up to the kitchen.

To his surprise, he saw the travel cooler, lid open, on the floor by the refrigerator. Sybil was making sandwiches. Jason, Remy, and Ayla were clustered at the breakfast table, enjoying blueberry pancakes with maple syrup. Jason was wearing a day pack and scooting his feet back and forth on his skateboard as he ate.

"The book club was cancelled," Sybil said. "I can go to yoga tomorrow. We'll need jackets. It'll be sunny up there, but cool. I checked."

Seth could hardly believe this change of fortune. He said nothing and tucked into breakfast, exultant.

***

Numberless other families had chosen to spend this sunny Easter day on the Parkway, too, for Seth ran into traffic before he got to the entry at Tuggle's Gap. All the scenic overlooks and designated picnic locations were full. Absorbed by their phones, neither Jason nor Ayla noticed. Remy had to go to the bathroom. Seth found a place to pull off and Sybil opened both her door and the rear passenger door to hide Remy. A police officer on a thunderous motorcycle pulled up to warn Seth he was in a 'no parking' area. It was an awkward moment.

"Where can we park?" Seth asked, doing his best to block the officer's view.

"I'd get off the parkway altogether if I was you. It's worse up ahead. There's a music festival."

The officer roared away. Sybil groaned.

"How was I supposed to know?" Seth protested.

"You weren't. You *never* are. Because you never plan ahead."

"Not true!"

"You just go la, la, la through life as if everything will work out just *fine*."

Seth stopped the car. "Damn it!" he said, striking the steering wheel with the flat of his hand and hating himself for this outburst in front of his children.

"What's up?" said Jason.

"I'm hot back here," said Ayla.

Sybil turned up the air conditioning and directed the dash vents toward the back seat. "Let's go home."

Glumly, Seth got off at the next exit, marking the miserable end to his lovely vision of a happy family outing. Fittingly, the sky clouded over.

Sybil tipped her seat back and closed her eyes.

Seth drove without thinking, numb to his surroundings. Somewhere on a winding road through woods and fields the car sputtered and lost power. The *check engine* light blinked on.

"Are we going to crash?" asked Remy.

Sybil came awake at once and gripped the dashboard.

Seth leaned forward, as if this would help, and pumped the gas. The car jerked, coughed, popped, and expired. Seth coasted to a stop on a gravel turn out.

"Waz up?" said Jason.

"Where are we?" asked Ayla.

"This is scary," said Remy.

"I thought you said you just had the car worked on," said Sybil.

Seth closed his eyes, breathed a silent prayer, and turned the key. He pumped the gas. He tried again. Nada. Nothing. Any more would kill the battery.

Sybil shuffled in her wallet, pulled out her AAA card and dialed the number. She put the phone to her ear.

Seth crossed his fingers.

She dialed again, then dropped the phone in her lap. "Dead. No coverage out here."

Everyone was profoundly silent.

"Could be just the fuel pump," Seth said, with a casual authority he did not feel. "Like my old van. After a few minutes it would fire right up."

Jason popped his door open and coasted away on his skateboard. Seth wished he could do the same. Jason did not get far before a sudden rain pelted him. He rushed back to the car and squeezed inside.

Rain mixed with hail pounded the hood and roof.

"This is fun," said Ayla.

"I'm hungry," said Remy.

Seth rubbed his temples.

Sybil turned in her seat and took Remy's hand. "Jason, reach back and open the cooler.

Jason moved his skateboard so he could turn.

"Don't put that dirty thing in my lap!" said Ayla.

"It's not dirty, it's *seasoned.*"

"Please!" said Seth, "do as your mother says."

"Ayla, pass out the paper plates," Sibyl instructed. "Jason, set the blueberry muffins to one side and get out the sandwiches. Fizzy waters and yogurt cups next."

Grudgingly, Seth relaxed. Sybil had even included lemon squares, his favorite. "My God!" he exclaimed, "you're a miracle worker!"

The children murmured their agreement.

Seth was almost gleeful. Maybe his planned family outing had been a bust, but it had led to this un-likely adventure together, which would be more memorable by far. He felt vindicated, though he dared not say this. He simply turned to Sibyl and smiled.

"Did I ever tell," she said, sipping her fizzy water, "about the time I almost ran away with Emerson Dark?"

His smile evaporated. His heart sank. What in the world had provoked his wife to open this locked door now? He shook his head as if drawing a blank. "Who?"

"The '60's folksinger!" burst out Ayla. "You didn't know, Dad?"

Seth did know, very well he knew. He had aped Emerson Dark in college, affecting, poorly, his rich baritone voice; struggling to imitate his haunting, poetic lyrics; diligently practicing, with only middling success, his nimble guitar playing. "Look," he said, "maybe you can tell me about this some other time."

"No, no!" cried out the children together, "Tell us!"

Sibyl put her drink in the cup holder and stared out the windshield as if seeing into the past. "My roommate bought tickets to see him. Then her *boyfriend* called so she went home that weekend. I felt totally abandoned. But I had the ticket, so I went by myself." She put her sandwich down. "It was at the *Chicory Coffee House*." She turned to Seth. "Remember that place?"

"Sort of." In fact, it had been his favorite hangout: comfortably run-down, with good beer.

"His look captured me," said Sibyl, turning away from Seth again. "He was a strong, well-built man, but he came across as *gentle*. His high cheek bones and long ponytail sure didn't hurt, either."

Seth was acutely aware of his own look-a-like

features and thinning hair.

"He took his time getting comfortable on stage, bantering with the audience. But the moment his fingers pulled a chord from his beat-up guitar, and he began to sing in his deep, rich voice, I was gone. Just gone!" She lay a hand on Seth's shoulder. "He really *got* women."

"I get it!" Seth said, leaning away from her.

In the back seat, Jason, Ayla, and Remy leaned forward, eager and fearful to hear more. It was like a cloak around their parents' marriage had lifted, revealing two persons they didn't know and who had once upon a time been separate from each other. It was weird.

"After he left the stage, I just sat there, stunned. The whole place cleared out and I hardly noticed. I went out the back door by accident, and there he was! Emerson Dark, *in the flesh*, with his battered guitar slung over his shoulder. He was looking at a piece of paper. When he heard the door slam shut behind me, he looked up. 'I'm lost!' he said. Even his speaking voice was musical. 'I was supposed to meet some friends.'"

"He gave me the paper. Written on it was the address of the old Swenson place. You remember, don't you, Seth?"

He did, of course. It was better known as *The Wild Farm* in those days. He'd dropped acid out there. Once in the barn hay loft with a crazy chick from Florida. But this liaison between his wife and the handsome, charismatic Emerson Dark had clearly been in a different register, still vividly memorable to her, even though the incident must have taken place forty-some years ago.

     House of Poetry

"So, I drove him out there," Sibyl continued. "We talked and laughed the whole way. There was a party going on when we got there. I didn't know anybody, and he didn't want to get sucked into that scene, so we went out on the back porch. The moon was just coming up, and you could see the river—like molten silver. We walked into the field and he pointed out constellations: Cassiopeia, the Seven Sisters, Leo the Lion. He said, 'I can feel a song coming on.'"

Sibyl put her hands together as if in prayer and held them to her face. "He sang a few bars."

Seth sat rigid as an effigy, acutely aware of their hushed children in the back seat.

"He asked if I'd ever seen a colt being born. Said he needed help with some fence-mending. Asked if I could learn to drive a tractor. 'Come to my farm with me,' he said."

Seth wanted to jump out of the car and run away down the road.

"Until Emerson's invitation that night, I knew what my future was going to be: teaching degree, marriage, a warm house with happy children." She fiddled with her purse. "For a moment, I didn't know what to do, or even who I was!"

Sibyl took Seth's hand. He wished he had the nerve to jerk it away. But he craved her touch.

"You're such a good man," she said. "Trustworthy. Reliable. I'm very happy in our life together. Really I am."

Seth suffered through her compliments.

Sibyl lifted his hand up and over the seat. "Remy, Ayla, Jason--give me your hands, too." They held out their hands to her as if they had been asked to dance, and she linked them all together with her own and Seth's. "Listen to your heart. Life is so brief!"

A hawk sailed low across the road and landed deftly in a tree as the sky brightened.

"Yo, dad!" said Jason, "why don't you try the car again?"

Everyone released their hands.

Seth stirred in his seat, thankful for a task. He drew a deep breath and turned the key. Without hesitation, the engine sprang to life.

The children cheered.

Seth rolled the window down, taking in the fresh air. He turned to Sibyl. All these years, he had just accepted her as his natural companion, a practically inevitable union. It was strange to think that but for her choice, he might not have been in her life at all.

"Touch," he said, with a sheepish smile, "it's all in the touch."

She leaned toward him and they kissed, joining lips to exclamations of "Gross!" "Eugh!" "Stop!"

Seth relished their exclamations as he drove into a burst of sunlight.

Baptism

MOTHER ARGUED FOR BAPTISM BY SPRIN-KLING; father held with immersion. Their disagreement worried me as a child; by high school graduation I had abandoned not only baptism but every other tenet of their Christianity. Father, ever hopeful, urged me to apply to his alma mater, Rock of Ages, and at least consider the ministry as a vocation. He promised in exchange to pay my tuition for the first year. Surprised by his generosity and eager to prove I could attend and yet remain immune to his pleas, I accepted. On a crisp morning in September he drove me to the bus station, where he took hold of me by the shoulders. "I don't know how you lost your faith, son, but God has not lost faith in you."

I shrugged in response but waved as he drove away.

On the ride north I studied the map of Chicago only to discover when I arrived that the city was vastly larger and more complicated than the map indicated. I did not find campus until after dark, and only after having been twice propositioned by men offering to take me in for the night. Due to a mix-up, my dormitory room was already occupied, and I was obliged to sleep in a study lounge. The next day a kindly administrator took me to an off-campus apartment just west of LaSalle Street usually reserved for juniors and seniors. In the evening, I walked all the way to the lakefront, where the brilliant lights of the city ended abruptly in a great expanse of dark water.

Rock of Ages touted itself as a "Christ-centered liberal arts college," and required students and faculty to sign a pledge of abstinence from alcohol, dancing, movies, card-playing, and membership in secret societies. Neither this pledge nor the curvilinear wall around campus could prevent cultural shifts from seeping in, along with weed, magic mushrooms, rock music, *Siddhartha*. A tall missionary's son with wavy hair who hailed from California gleefully proclaimed the world was "absurd." I was embarrassed that I had not known this but did not say so. Searching for antecedents in the library I turned up riches: Blake's *The Marriage of Heaven and Hell*, which so thrilled me I stole it.

The professors to my chagrin were good, especially the amiable gentleman with wispy hair who taught Romantic Lit. and dwelt glowingly on Tolkien's use of *myth*, enunciating the word as if it were a magic spell. One day as I stood up at the end of class, my *Marriage* slipped out from among the other books and fell to the floor. Heather, whose long, loose hair I had frequently admired, gracefully stooped and picked it up, saying as she handed it back, *"if the doors of perception were cleansed everything would appear to—*woman--*as it is, infinite."* Her substitution struck me with a mingled note of boldness and heresy. She invited me outside, where we sat on a small stone bench under a ginkgo tree and talked Blake for an hour. She knew more about him than I did, had toiled through his prophetic writings, and even seen some of his etched copper plates at the Tate in London. I was smitten! As she stood up to go she said, "would you like to come with me to church on Sunday?" If anyone else had asked, my answer would have been an emphatic "no," but in the light of her smile I accepted.

It wasn't just her, it turned out, but six other Rock of Ages students as well—Raymond, who might have been her boyfriend, Jenny, Thomas, Rupert, Cline, and India, or "Indie." The "church" she spoke of was a basement room below the campus chapel. When the group of us arrived, some forty people were already sitting quietly with bowed heads in semi-circular rows of folding chairs. We took our seats in silence. Heather beside me knit her hands together in her lap. I didn't know what to do with my hands and was against bowing my head, so sat straight and waited uncomfortably for the service to begin.

Finally, a sturdily built man with swept back hair got to his feet, a large Bible open in his hand. He did not begin with words of welcome and seemed hardly to notice people were present. I had often listened to my father preach and came grudgingly to appreciate the care with which he prepared and delivered a sermon. Quite often he read portions straight from his prepared text. This man, with eyes closed, spoke haltingly, as if he did not know what he would say next. He was like a blind man tapping his way along a word at a time. Everyone around me, including Heather, was still and silent as if they were tapping along in unison immediately behind him. A thought came suddenly into my mind: *this man is a false prophet, do not be deceived!* The thought dismayed me, for it seemed not to be my own, but my father's. In reaction, I willed myself to listen without criticism, and fell into step: tap, tap, tap. Abruptly the service ended.

Shaken, I stood up slowly. Heather put her hand on my arm. Her touch signaled to me that I belonged. I went to church with her and the others again the following Sunday and then regularly on both Sunday and Wednesday evenings. I was baptized in the Spirit with the laying on of hands, without any water at all, an action I could hardly explain to myself and would never have dared admit to my father. Church became the axle upon which my life turned.

***

In the spring, I received an unexpected letter from Matthew, my best friend from high school. After our junior year he had moved with his parents back to Polestar in southern Georgia, so his father could run the family's lumber business. From childhood Matt aspired to become a builder, hoping family connections in Polestar would ensure this. These connections had proven to be a millstone, he wrote. But he was not giving up: "Did Frank Lloyd Wright surrender to his critics? Hell no! He wrote his manifesto, *The Future of Architecture*, as I shall write mine one day." Matthew's conclusion was jolting: "Since my odds of success are far better in a city of three million than in this outpost of rednecks numbering no more than thirteen thousand, I am coming to Chicago. Look for me in five days."

Rock of Ages had strict rules about overnight guests of either sex, even in off-campus housing, let alone a rebellious high school buddy with zero interest in religion who might be expecting to move in with me. I had no idea how he had gotten my address, and hoped, with some shame, that he wouldn't be able to find me. But he did. Not five days later, but four, on an otherwise beautiful day in late April, mere hours after my landlady's rosebush began to bloom. Coming home from class in the afternoon, I saw a scratched and dented VW bus parked at the curb. Matthew was on the porch step, looking as though he had just come from a jobsite. His bushy hair was flecked with sawdust. To one side like a faithful dog was his worm-drive circular saw, and on the other side a toolbelt and hammer. Seeing me, he stood up and leaned insolently against the porch post, as if he owned the place. He deftly lit a cigarette, took a long drag, and with an expression which was a mixture of compliment and derision said, "So, a scholar now, are we? *Feckless.*"

"I didn't ask you to come here."

Ignoring my rebuke he nodded toward his bus. "Trojan and I have already scored in your windy city. As of one o'clock this afternoon, I am a sub-contractor for Imperial Construction Company. Does renovation jobs all over the South Side." He stubbed out his cigarette on the post and flicked it into the rosebush. "I need a hand. You in?"

Of course I was not in, I told him. He might mock school but I didn't. My deeper objection was church, which I dared not mention. I could not work his schedule because I was a member of a body of believers compelled to be present for every service. Only when gathered together could the Word be revealed in our midst through the pastor. Rumors about the church so disturbed Rock of Ages administrators that we were forced to meet off campus. Faculty wives had initiated prayer circles in which they spoke our names aloud and petitioned God to save us from the devil. These rumors and fearful prayers only strengthened the bonds among us. We were a people wandering in the wilderness. When, oh Lord, would we come into the promised land of understanding? Through Christ on the cross. Not by assent, but experience. Not through belief in a Jesus crucified two millennia ago, but through the lived experience of ourselves being joined to the body of Christ crucified. Service after service, week after week, we hung on the cross, longing for Resurrection. Though painful to hear, the Word was fruit to our lips; bread to our being; a mystery impossible—impermissible—to explain to anyone else. Matthew in particular.

I distracted his question with a tour of campus. He noted with approval the slate roofs, copper gutters, and leaded glass of the chapel windows. Back at my apartment I fed him a scholar's supper of bread and soup, and he collapsed on the couch and shortly fell asleep. He was gone before I got up in the morning and did not return until dusk. His presence was not the interruption I had feared: I went on with my studies and church, he with his work. This pattern continued to the end of the school year. By then I had decided to stay on at Rock of Ages, much to my father's delight. I took a part time job mopping floors in the dining hall and enrolled in summer classes.

One afternoon I came home to find a dusty compact with missing bumper parked at the curb, and Matthew slumped on the porch.

"You're home early," I said. "Where's Trojan?"

"Broke down. On the Eisenhower Expressway. Had to be towed. The guy that runs the shop gave me

     House of Poetry

that loaner to drive."

"Some loaner. He must like you."

Matthew lit a cigarette. "I got so pissed off this last job, I took the goddamn twisted studs back to the lumberyard and picked out my own. Charged 'em to the company. Tore out the stud wall and started over." He struck the porch post with the flat of his hand. "Then the *crook* owner showed up. Wanted to know why I'd built the wall on 16" centers rather than 24. I told him I was done building shit and cutting corners. I got religious about it, man."

"I bet he liked your sermon."

He stubbed out his cigarette and pitched it into the rosebush. "Fired my ass. Said if he found me doing work *anywhere* in the city he would sue me down to the last dime. And confiscate my tools."

"So you drove off in righteous indignation and Trojan broke down."

"Hell!" he said, stomping the porch with his boot, "now what? Back to Polestar, I guess. Damn it!"

I'd never seen him so downcast. "Who's *feckless* now?" I said, hoping to get a rise out of him.

He didn't stir.

"Take me for a ride in that crappy loaner. Let's see if that guy has got Trojan fixed." I walked over to the Toyota, struggled with the door handle, got in on the driver's side, then found I could not roll the window down. I sat in the hot, cramped vehicle for several minutes before Matthew came down off the porch and got in.

The car started and died twice.

"Nice rig."

I braced my feet against the floorboard as Matthew shifted hard through the gears, ran a red light, and merged onto the Dan Ryan, weaving through heavy traffic. He got off on the Eisenhower and exited at Ashland.

"Drive much?" I said, loosening my grip on the dashboard.

We passed Malcolm X College, proclaimed in huge, black letters.

I looked at Matthew. "Where is this place?"

He grinned at me. "You, *feckless*."

We went on for another six blocks. The street was badly in need of repair, and so were the sooty buildings we passed. Men—all of them black—stood talking, smoking, or leaning on cars. Matthew coasted through the traffic light at Leverage Street and came to a stop.

"You coming?" he said and got out.

I jimmied with my door handle, again without success, and slid out Matthew's side. From the Eisenhower, adjacent but below street level, issued an ugly, tuneless drone, a river of noise, whose wind stirred in the weeds and scrubby trees clinging to life along a chain-link fence stuck with plastic bags and old papers. Heat radiated with oven-like intensity from the dirty streets and brick walls. The hot sun glared sharply from the cracked windshields, damaged fenders, dented hubcaps of dilapidated cars parked in a bunch on the corner and along the curb. All was harsh, coarse, grating, soiled.

Matthew strode boldly up the broad, oil-spotted concrete apron toward an L-shaped building emblazoned with the words, "Rubio Auto Repair." Even the lunge of two German Shepherd guard dogs, barking madly and straining at their heavy chains, did not distract him. I hurried to catch up. A casual half circle of black men were talking and joking with a trim, swarthy man. His curly black hair and beard shone. A gold earring flashed. Feet planted a shoulder's width apart, hands loose and ready at his sides, he radiated alert vitality. Then he laughed. Threw back his head and laughed, open-mouthed. In a setting which to me crushed the very idea of laughter. I was mesmerized.

Matthew went boldly right up to this man and began talking with him. They pointed at Trojan, parked up against the building, hemmed in by two dusty, dented cars. A bay door was open beside this cluster, with a car up on the lift. There was so much stuff underneath there was no way the car could be let down. I was distracted by a slender black boy on a banana seat bicycle who performed a wheelie just across the street while two men standing at a doorway lifted their pool cues in salute.

Matthew came back to me. Two steps away he hopped in the air. "Hot damn!" he exclaimed. Shading his eyes with one hand, he gestured grandly and shouted over the Eisenhower traffic noise. "The whole block is going to be razed to the ground! Those brick houses up the street, Rubio's business, *everything*. He pointed toward the brick building across Leverage Street, where I'd just watched the boy perform his wheelie. "Rubio needs *somebody* to turn the ground floor of *that* building into a new auto shop, then move his *whole* operation from *here* over to *there*."

He lit a cigarette. "I told him *we* are that somebody."

"I already have a job mopping floors."

"Not anymore. I told Rubio you are my electrician."

I nearly fell over. "Are you kidding me? I don't know anything about electricity!"

"*Feckless*. Better learn."

He held up a set of keys, jingling them. "Rubio gave me something else to drive." He strode around the side of the building as if he'd been working there for weeks. Under a withered tree sat a dusty, turquoise Cadillac convertible, with white interior. We folded back the ripped top and got in. Once on the expressway, Matthew gunned it. The Caddy stuttered a moment and then leaped forward, as if suddenly recovering its days of glory, and we promptly dubbed it "The Emperor." Matt howled to the hot sky for all he was worth and I howled, too.

I resigned my job mopping floors, snuck Blake's *Marriage* back onto the library shelf, and bought *The Practical Guide to Electrical Wiring*, which I studied as if my life depended on it, which in fact it could.

Two days later we returned to Rubio's, and with Trojan back in running order drove to a lumber yard and bought materials to begin work. Our task was absurdly beyond my experience and even Matthew's, but his confidence was boundless. To expedite the work, Rubio offered to let Matthew and I live rent-free in one of his houses, 324 Leverage, which in its day must have been a handsome residence and was only five doors down the street from the corner building we would be renovating into a new shop. Most of the houses on both sides of the block belonged to Rubio. Outsiders would have called him a slumlord, but for that neighborhood he was like the godfather. He said to us, "if anybody gives you trouble, you tell them you are my sons." We understood without his saying so that he had allies, and that the neighborhood knew it. Not so much as one word in anger was ever raised against us. The locus of activity was his shop.

Meanwhile, demolition crews and equipment, notably an impressive crane with a heavy wrecking ball, had rumbled into the neighborhood, and starting at Adams Street had begun working their way south along the west side of Leverage, reducing each house to a field of rubble picked over by brick collectors. With the ever-present noise and dust of this destruction as pressure, and because we were still months away from completion of Rubio's new shop and emptying out his old one, I withdrew from Rock of Ages well before the end of summer, which greatly disappointed my father. For the first time I felt sorry for him, and even apologized.

But I had not discontinued my education, as he charged or I supposed. Rubio's shop was immersion in a new reality. Everybody came there to do business, air complaints, beg money, hang out. He was strictly a cash business; his bank was the thick wad of bills in his pocket. Frequently in the mornings a bread truck would stop by. After chatting amiably with the driver, Rubio would buy an enormous bag of day-old French bread and walk down the street handing out loaves. Nearly every afternoon, a cavalcade of colorful characters came by: cops, each one a half-size larger than an ordinary man and always in pairs; vendors of stolen merchandise, who showed up as frequently as the cops though at different times, displaying their wares on the hoods or in the trunks of their cars; Sonny, a mysterious boulder of a man who hauled cast iron tubs with a rope down the steep staircases of soon-to-be demolished houses to sell for scrap; Mary, the prostitute, thin and sharp-witted, boldly teasing Rubio, who laughed and teased back; Aaron, voluble and animated, who it was rumored had been shot in the head but showed up a few days later, his head wrapped in bandages, as energetic as before; Bone, in his signature blue silk suit and broad-brimmed hat, who allegedly was pimping his own sister. Matthew and I became characters ourselves, or tried to be, donning headscarves like pirates, and piercing each other's ear for a gold stud, in imitation of Rubio.

Among all these characters, and others, Willie G. stood out. Trim, handsome, and blessed with an athletic grace of movement, he took boundless pleasure in simply being himself. Doing a quick little two-step on the sidewalk, he would bob and weave for a moment like a boxer, then stand still and smile. A dozen or more children would flock around him, pulling on his arms until at last, with mock resignation, he would agree to be chased. Quick and agile, he kept just a hand's breadth out of the children's reach, dodging this way and that, doubling back, spinning around and back-pedaling, grinning broadly and clapping his hands, as the children rushed after him, screaming with delight.

I struggled to continue attending church, but could not sit long without dozing off, no matter how urgent the Word. At least twice, to my intense embarrassment, Heather had to wake me. How could I sleep through our crucifixion? Embarrassment turned to shame; I hesitated to return lest it happen again. Going intermittently was worse than not going at all, so I quit altogether. Guilt accumulated. I was a reprobate,

    House of Poetry

a traitor, as weak and faithless as Pilgrim fallen into the Slough of Despond. But I was also free; free from the interminable dying on the cross. Rubio's neighborhood was dying enough. We were working across the street from the rubble and dust of it. From the front room of 317 Leverage, Bone's "headquarters"--void of furniture except for a few battered chairs--I could see out the front window the wrecking ball at work across the street. Yet the neighborhood on this side pulsed on, resistant to destruction. It was a mystery to me, this conjugation of dissolution and vitality.

I could never have spoken about any of this to church members, especially Heather, and only hoped she would remember me no more. To myself, though, I argued that I was not faithless but simply unable to heal the disconnect between church and street; between a spiritual realm of principalities and powers and living the pungent actuality of our days at Rubio's.

Willie G. often came down to the shop, at first just to watch us at work, and then to ask questions: growing up, did we have our own bed? Was there more than one bathroom? Did it have a shower? Did we have to share clothes? Was there a yard? How big? Did we cut the grass, or was somebody hired to do it? He was sure we must be brothers, even though we told him again and again we were not related and did not even live in the same state. Our world was as exotic to him as his world was to us.

His questions interfered with our work. Matthew grew so impatient one afternoon that he struck a heavy timber with the little sledge and burst out, "Dude! We've got a job to do here, can't you see? Get a life!"

Willie G. backed out of the shop without another word. Two weeks later we heard he'd gotten a job as a bellhop at the Drake Hotel on Michigan Avenue. One afternoon he showed up wearing a broad-brimmed black hat—broader than Bone's—with a silver band; trim, black pants with silver studs down the outside seams of both legs; a waist-length black jacket to match, with a row of silver stars across the back of the shoulders; a cardinal-red silken shirt open low on his chest, and a bright, yellow neck scarf. His black shoes were polished to a mirror finish.

"What are you, a bullfighter?" said Matthew.

"All you need is a cape," I said.

"Nah!" said Willie G. with a gleaming smile, "I don't need no cape. All I got to do is look at that big 'ol bull, and he lay *right* down." He spread out his hands, palms down, then clapped and laughed.

***

Winter was cold that year. Lake Michigan froze. Snow turned to ice. The gas-fired heater we had mounted above the bay doors of the new shop blew hot when it kicked on but left us even colder when it shut off. We bundled in heavy clothes, which made all our movements slow. Tools felt heavy and brittle. Demolition crews ceased work; only brick collectors persisted.

There were no flowers in the neighborhood to usher in spring but warmth returned, which was enough. We shed our coats and gloves and got back to work in earnest as the demolition crews crashed their way toward the old shop, house by house.

In June, fourteen months after Matthew and I

had begun working at Rubio's, I received a letter from Heather. She said she missed my company, talked about church, and invited me out to a 4th of July picnic at her family's property somewhere west of the city. "There's an old quarry, a magic spot," she wrote. "Bring your swimsuit!" Below her note was a carefully drawn map and directions leading to an oval shape marked with wavey lines. She had missed my company! I desperately wanted to go. But how? I had no vehicle, Matthew was possessive of Trojan, and I couldn't simply drive off in one of Rubio's old cars without some explanation. I kept my longing secret and counted down the days.

On July 3rd, we powered up the electric panel, tested the air compressor and hydraulic lift, plumbed the bathroom, and installed two deadbolts on the front door. In celebration, Rubio went to visit his lady friend in Hyde Park for two nights. Late in the morning on Independence Day, we removed from the old shop Rubio's phone with the ten-foot cord, his podium with the address book on top, and the sawed-off shotgun he kept hidden in the wall. This trinity of sacred objects we ceremoniously installed in the new shop, between the overhead doors and with a clear view of the street. Matthew and I stood together without speaking and gazed across Leverage at the old shop, once Rubio's bastion and now empty and desolate, bay doors gone, "Rubio Auto Repair" taken off the wall, and the wrecking ball on its cable dangling ominously over the roof. I felt as though an age had gone by since that first sweltering hour when I had witnessed Matthew stride boldly toward the distinctive figure of Rubio standing so trim and alert and joyous in that half circle of black men. We had arrived at the end of that beginning. I felt both accomplished and empty.

Matthew pulled out a cigarette and began to smoke. "What now?"

I watched him a moment, considering. "How about a picnic?"

"What, here?"

It was a funny moment. A picnic in the rubble. We shared a laugh. I told him about Heather, and her letter. Nothing about church.

"You got it hard for that chick."

I turned away from his scrutiny.

"You, *feckless*!" He slapped his trouser leg. "Hell, yes, we'll go to your picnic."

I slapped my trouser, too. "Let's lock up the dogs and go." This was always the last piece of business on any working day: locking up Pharoah and Caesar in the shop, with two cans of dogfood for them to fight over and tear open.

As Matthew pulled the door closed, he jingled keys at me. "We're taking the Emperor."

We rushed to the house, cleaned up and changed clothes, and sprinted back to where the Emperor sat under its withered tree. We folded the top back and settled into the still swank though cracked white leather seats. The old turquoise Caddy fired right up, as if eager to carry us toward adventure. What an entrance we would make at Heather's picnic! Matthew backed the Emperor over the curb and into the street just as Willie G. came easy down the street in his bull fighter's garb: black suit, red shirt, yellow scarf, broad hat, gleaming shoes. He did look fine.

I grabbed the windshield and stood up. "Willie G!" I called, waving, "Come on to a picnic with us!"

Matthew stopped the Emperor and I got out, folding the front seat forward and holding the door open. "Get in!"

Willie G. came up to the car, his smile nearly as broad as his hat. "Picnic, say you?"

"Out in the country! To swim."

His smile faded. "I don't have no *swimsuit*."

I shrugged. "Neither do we."

As lithe as a gymnast Willie G. hopped over the side of the car and into the middle of the back seat all in one motion. "We goin' or stayin'?"

Off we went, and right away I pictured us arriving: Heather running up, excited to see me but a little shocked by the funky old Cadillac convertible with a cool dude from the ghetto in the back seat.

"How far is this picnic?" Willie G. shouted, as we got onto the Eisenhower going west.

"Not so far. Maybe thirty miles!" I shouted back.

"*Thirty?*"

The way he said it made it seem as if we were on a journey to a foreign country.

"It'll be beautiful out there," I said, turning in my seat to face him as he leaned forward. "No buildings, no streets, no traffic, just *nature!*"

He said nothing and fell back against the seat with a stone-faced expression. He squinted his eyes against the wind, his yellow scarf pulling at his neck, the tails streaming out behind him. His broad hat he clutched to his chest like a breastplate. I began to feel that it had been a terrible idea to ask him to come along to this picnic. Terrible to be going with Matthew, too, given that I had told him nothing about church. Terrible to arrive in this beat-up old car with its rusted-out muffler. I nearly told Matthew to turn back, but he had lit himself a cigarette and switched on the radio, such as it was.

Following Heather's directions, we drove south on the Dan Ryan and then southwest on the Stevenson Expressway before exiting north on two lane Route 53. Finally, we bumped down off the asphalt onto a dirt road which passed by a marsh, went through a stand of oak trees, came around a bend, and ended beside a cluster of crabapple trees. Two other cars were parked nearby. We followed a winding footpath to the top of a low hill and stopped. There below us lay the quarry pond, glittering in the sun, the water a beautiful jade green. On the far side, a deep field of long grasses rippled beguilingly in a gentle, shifting wind.

It didn't matter that we had no swimsuits. Jenny bobbed in the water, her breasts showing. Raymond, deeply tanned except for his white buttocks, bent down to touch the water, and then jumped in. And Heather, shapely Heather, ascending to a high rock, pointed her hands in the air and dove, disappearing into the water as smoothly as a dolphin.

I cannot recall walking down to the pond, or undressing, or getting in the water. As though I had been transported through the air, clothes evaporating off my body as I flew, I found myself splashing excitedly in that bright, chilly, sparkling water with my church friends as though we were children in a huge baptismal fount. I felt cleansed of guilt; I was the lost sheep gathered back into the fold! Matthew, his characteristic sneer gone, splashed right along with us. We were all of us together as if reborn, naked in a world made new.

     House of Poetry

Heather popped out of the water near me like a mermaid. "Hello, stranger!" she said, slicking back her long golden hair.

I was foolishly happy.

She took my hand and drew me into deeper water where we caught hold of a slippery log and tried to get on. Soon the whole group had paddled out to join us. The log spun this way and that, frustrating our efforts and prompting laughter. Somehow we got ourselves organized, paired up on either side and on a count of three boosted out of the water. Heather, at the front of the log and opposite me, vaulted into the air with graceful strength, flung out her leg like a dancer, and firmly bestrode the log as if she were our captain. I clambered up behind her. Pearls of water slid glistening down her strong back. Matthew, sitting stern-most, called out a cadence, and we scooped at the water in unison, slowly propelling our log boat toward the further shore as if making for the promised land. In that moment, that one rapturous moment, my life at Rubio's and my life in the church were knitted together; the world as it is and the world to be were joined in marriage, one flesh, wholly present to each other. Rapture!

Then I saw Willie G. He sat motionless, fully clothed, nearly hidden in the tall, wind-swept grasses crowding the shore ahead. He'd drawn himself up in a ball, his chin on his knees, his dark face in shadow under that broad hat. I felt as though I were seeing him for the first time, and that I was seeing what he saw: a young, beautiful, nude white woman, her body glistening in the sun, propelling herself through the sparkling jade waters toward him, a black man hiding in the weeds. A sight mesmerizing and terrible, from which he could not withdraw his eyes but was forbidden to see. A sight which once upon a time would have gotten him lynched.

***

We left the picnic early and drove back to the city in silence. I tried to apologize but Willie G. sat with head bowed or looked out the window. I gave up, repenting the afternoon in private, and hoping that would suffice.

I was mistaken. Two days later he came to our house. I was packing my suitcase; I'd called for a cab to take me to the airport. Matthew was down at the new shop loading up Trojan with his tools.

I was afraid I knew what Willie G. wanted but opened the door anyway.

"What's her name?"

I looked at my watch.

"Just tell me her name, can you?"

"Heather, I think."

He repeated her name. Twice.

"Look, I've got to get packed."

"I know, I know. Just give me Heather's phone number and I'll go."

I was not about to give him her phone number. I mean, suppose Willie G. called her, what would she think? What would she think of me?

"I don't know what it is, right off."

"Well just take a look, can you?"

"I don't know where her phone number is, okay? I don't call her that often. Hardly ever." In fact, I'd never called her. The reason being I was too shy, which

    House of Poetry

was embarrassing.

Willie G. did not give up. He wanted to know where she lived, at least. Or anyway her address, so he could write her. Just write her, that was all. Or maybe I could write something for him, and see that she got it? Could I do that?

I told him no, again and again, and tried to be polite about it, I really did, until finally I just shut the door on him. The cab was going to arrive any minute and no way did I want to miss my flight. I still had some packing to do! The cabbie honked when he pulled up to the curb, but I peeked out the window to see if Willie G. was still around, before hustling out the door, down the steps and into the cab, pulling my suitcase in after me. I had the cabbie stop at the shop, where Matthew and I shook hands. We promised each other to stay in touch. Not long afterwards he died in a car wreck, his manifesto unwritten and his millions unrealized. Heather moved out to San Francisco somewhere. The church pastor suffered a stroke, rendering him unable to speak.

***

In the years that followed, I made a point of visiting Rubio when I had business in the Chicago area. He would bring out a pair of hand-rolled Italian cigars, light them from an acetylene torch, and we would smoke and talk. I always asked about Willie G. The news was worse every time: he quit his job as a bellhop; he'd taken to drinking; he'd been arrested for breaking into a grocery store; he was a dopehead and couldn't be trusted around the shop because he stole anything he

could get his hands on; doctors had amputated his right
foot, then his other leg, but that only slowed the diabe-
tes which finally killed him. Too late, I wished I'd taken
the time to visit him before he died. But would he have
wanted me to see him? Could I have borne the sight?

The cherished visits with Rubio ended after his
struggle with an intruder who shot him. He was taken
to a veterans' hospital where he endured eighteen sur-
geries. By providence or happenstance, I was just west
of the city when I found out. When I got to his room,
his sons told me he was due back any moment from yet
another surgery. We waited together in silence. The el-
evator door opened and two orderlies pushed a gurney
toward us. I was shocked to see Rubio prone and mo-
tionless--he who had been for me the epitome of vigor
and radiant vitality. He was as shocked to see me. "I've
done everything to stay alive," he said, flashing a smile.
I took his hand and bent low to his ear. "I love you, Rubio," I whispered.

After that, I could not bear to go anywhere
near the city, and didn't, for almost twenty years. But
vivid memories of my time at Rubio's, with Matthew,
renovating the old pool hall into a shop and witness-
ing so much life, were ever-present. How could I forget
Sonny, Mary, Aaron, Bone and Pee Wee, and everybody
else, especially Willie G.?

One spring day, coming up Interstate 65 from
Indianapolis, I made up my mind to take a look, so went
straight into the city and took 90 West, the Eisenhower.
A shiver of anticipation went through me when I got
off at Paulina and continued west on Van Buren. Things
had changed. Malcolm X College was no longer simply
an outpost, but a large campus busy with students. Van

 House of Poetry

Buren was better paved, here and there, at least. The sooty old buildings I remembered were interrupted by sections of clean, well-brushed apartments.

At the traffic light for Leverage, I slowed. Rubio's shop was gone. Gone! A car honked behind me, I turned the corner, gawking at the void, drove up the street, parked and got out, numb. No dented cars crowded along the curb. No trash on the street. Except for the dull sound of the Eisenhower, the place was as quiet as a suburb and void of people. No families on their porches, no teenagers on the sidewalk, no fruit wagon ringed with buyers. Every slum house on the block had been so thoroughly refurbished I had to look for the address numbers to identify them and still could not be certain. Was this the one where Matthew and I had lived? That the one where Bone and his cronies congregated? Across the street, where I had witnessed house after house demolished into dust and debris, a security fence ringed a block-sized athletic field, as quiet as a cemetery.

Slowly, I walked down to Rubio's corner, preparing myself for a closer look. There was nothing to see but a square of meager grass, with an arrangement of rocks in the middle and a crudely lettered sign: "Clean up after your pet." How could a space so small have once been the site of so much vivid activity, day after day, for years? I was desperate to exclaim my consternation to somebody; it was too great for me to bear alone. Down the street came a black woman in a long coat, carrying a shopping bag. When she got close, I babbled out my disbelief. I was sure she thought I must be crazy. Could I coherently express, in the one minute before the signal light changed, to this perfect stranger and sudden confessor, the packed history of this place for me, its pitiable grave baptized in the sprinkled, sprayed, or squirted urine of household pets?

She was patient, did not flee, but listened, watching me closely. "Have a blessed day," she said, before crossing the street into her own life again.

I turned back up the street to my car. For a moment, I imagined that I saw Willie G., dressed in his bullfighter's outfit. He danced a neat two-step on the sidewalk, bobbed and weaved for a moment like a boxer, then stood still and smiled. Children swarmed around him, and he, laughing, dodged and twisted away as he led them, joyful and screaming, down the street and around a corner out of sight.

     House of Poetry

House of Poetry

JUDITH STANDARD WAS CALLED UP TO THE new President's office, told by the Executive Secretary to wait, then ushered in to see an assistant, who smiled, folded his hands, and thanked Judith for her "years of service to this great university." Someone from Personnel Services explained, in an apologetic tone, that she had three options—severance package, full retirement, or transition to an "honorary post." She was to vacate her office by the end of the day. Shocked, she demanded an explanation. "So grieve it," said the assistant, "if you wish to waste your time."

Numb, she took the backstairs down to the second floor; a pair of grave campus police officers stood waiting at her door. She acknowledged their presence with a nod, as if nothing were amiss, went inside and sat down at her desk. She enjoyed for the last time her beautiful view of the Grand Commons, around which were arranged the principal academic buildings, all of them built in the imposing Collegiate Gothic style. A lone pigeon, buffeted by chilly autumn winds, canted its way through the air. A gust of oak leaves swept along the ground.

She had given the best part of her life to this university. Apparently that had not counted for much. She thought dismissal or demotion without explanation was confined to the business world, not present in the academy. Not here at Standolphus at least. Not to her. A crew from Moving and Hauling announced they were there to help load up her books and papers.

She chose transition to the "honorary post": Principal Archivist of the Standolphus Rare Books Collection, known on campus as FEFA, "First Editions by Forgotten Authors." A Vice President sent a confidential note. "Do us a favor down there, will you? Initiate a collection of 'underrepresented voices.' Nothing fancy. Budget tight. That's a good woman!"

She had not the least intention of obliging him. She wanted to be left alone. She was content to be forgotten, along with the FEFA authors, whose editions—first and otherwise—she browsed. She had the time; little was expected of her. She didn't report to anybody on a regular basis. She even had an assistant, Tubby Sanders. Tubby was a local, and more interested in gossip than books, but he had worked in FEFA for years. He knew the collection, handled paperwork, retrieved archival materials for the occasional researcher, and chatted amiably with the odd student. He was not interested in advancement. Nor did he like having a new boss looking over his shoulder, especially her, she found out.

This was insulting, of course. But she recognized opportunity. With so much time on her hands, she could at long last return to poetry, her first love. Administration had been a discouraging sidetrack, a long and enervating detour, the bending of her pliant personality toward serving the unbending demands of men in power. Too often it became merely secretarial, even the serving of coffee. Now her heart sang. A poet she would be again. Cozily hidden among aromatic old books in the back room she unlimbered her pen. For this work she nixed the computer, choosing to write in ink—no ballpoint, with its imperfect line—on 24 lb paper, 25% cotton. She had seen the ravages of time on poor paper.

Her only bother was Tubby, who would look in on her. "You need any help back here, darlin'?"

"No."

He leaned against the door frame, the next time. He was a heavy-set man, blocking her exit. "What is it you do back here, boss?"

She suspected he was reporting to somebody. "Working on a proposal."

"What sort of proposal?"

Judith put her pen down. "For a collection of under-represented voices."

"You mean like, bitch poets?"

She ought to have fired him on the spot. But she wasn't sure of her authority here. He was a long-term employee. More importantly, she didn't want to draw attention to her situation, which was otherwise good. Her poem was beginning to take shape. "Something like that."

***

On a bitter morning in early February, having penned what she hoped were worthy stanzas, she went out to the lobby to stretch her legs. Tubby, with his mug of coffee, was looking out the broad window. Snow was coming down hard. Across the library plaza, Judith could see the Grand Commons. Bertram Hall loomed up darkly. With its turreted tower and crenelated battlements, it was a commanding structure.

I am insurgent, she thought, *hear me breaking down your walls.* She was surprised at herself, but thrilled. She would get that line into the next stanza.

A long pickup truck drew up to the plaza curb; workmen, bundled against the cold, climbed out of the back, shovels in hand. They began clearing the steps of the university bookstore.

"I don't envy 'em," said Tubby, sipping his coffee.

The driver got out of the cab and with shovel in hand approached the entrance steps to FEFA. He wore a bill cap, which stuck out from beneath the hood of his coat like a beak. His long, thin beard whipped in the wind.

"That there's Grady Pentecost," said Tubby, lifting his mug.

"Pentecost! What a name."

"Well known, hereabouts. Goes way back."

Pentecost worked methodically, first clearing the landing up to the doors and then down the three steps one at a time. His shovel blade scraped on the stone. At the plaza level, he straightened, his bearded face in profile, and watched the men shoveling the bookstore steps. A certain stillness in the way he stood in the blowing snow held Judith's attention. Breaking the stillness, he walked over to the men at the bookstore steps and began shoveling. As they finished, a tractor with plowblade bumped up over the curb onto the plaza. Pentecost and the tractor driver consulted.

"He probably qualifies for your collection of *under-represented voices,*" Tubby said.

Judith hardly heard him. She was fixed on Pentecost. He beckoned his workmen back to the truck. For an instant, she was sure, he saw her looking at him out the window. Then he and his men drove off.

Tubby repeated himself.

Judith looked at him, sure he was mocking her.

"You think I'm nothing but an insolent rube, don't you?"

Judith didn't respond.

"Believe me or not, boss," he said, pouring his coffee into a potted plant by the door, "he's a poet, or claims to be. And crazy."

Judith went back to her desk and took up her pen again, but couldn't get on with her poem. "Pentecost!" she said aloud, relishing the syllables, "Pentecost." She pictured his face in profile again, with the high cheekbone and strong nose. A poet? Really? Against her better judgment she went out to the lobby again. Tubby was seated behind the front desk.

"It's still snowing," she said.

He looked up from some papers he was going through. "Don't worry, darlin'. He'll be back."

"Who?" she asked, in a voice so false she fled back to her desk in embarassment.

She dared go out front twice more. The first time a tractor was plowing the plaza again, and the second, workmen were salting the steps. But no Pentecost.

That day established her habit. She studiously kept at her poem, taking a turn through the lobby every so often to casually scan the plaza, trying to avoid Tubby's gaze. These turns became more frequent as her poem became more troublesome. As a pretext she even began drinking coffee though she hated the stuff Tubby made. Winter turned to spring. The snow melted away.

One sunny morning, Judith was cleaning her coffee cup with a damp paper towel. The poem had come to a dead stop. She'd lost the sense of where she was going with it.

"He's here, boss," said Tubby.

She dropped the coffee cup, which smashed on the floor. She ignored her embarassing accident and stared out the window. Pentecost and his crew, cloth sacks slung over their shoulders and long metal rods with sharpened tips in hand, spread out over the plaza, stabbing bits of paper and other debris with the rods, and depositing them in the sacks. Pentecost worked around the low bushes under the front windows of FEFA. On hands and knees, he diligently pulled out plastic bags, a soda can, torn newspaper.

"Such humble work!" thought Judith. Yet he applied himself with methodical industry. He paused, sat up perfectly still and lifted his eyes. Judith followed his gaze. In a tree, a small, quick bird, bright yellow, perched, bobbing, at the very tip of a branch.

"Go on out there and get down on your hands and knees with him, why don't you?" said Tubby. He eyed her brazenly.

She turned on her heel and hurried back to her desk in the back room, eager to get down her vivid impression of Pentecost. A sonnet emerged, which so pleased her she submitted it to the *Chestnut Review*. When she received an acceptance note, a thrill passed through her. She let go of all modesty and pictured herself a celebrated poet, crowned with plaudits, a PEN or Pulitzer. Of *course*, she would invite the President of Standolphus and his staff to the ceremony, with never a word of reproach to them in her acceptance speech.

She began to rebuild her big poem, with Pentecost at its core. Her fire for the work returned, and her need to see more of him. One afternoon he and his crew showed up carrying flats filled with small pots of flowers. They spread out, and setting down their flats, began tipping the flowers out of the pots and planting them. Pentecost worked at the large, oval bed near the center of the plaza. He pulled a trowel from his back pocket and got down on his knees.

"Introduce me," said Judith suddenly.

Tubby gave her a long look. "What, for a date?"

Judith turned on him. "The man works out here all the time to make our entryway attractive. The least I can do is thank him. As Director."

Tubby closed the visitors' log on the front desk, and put his coffee cup down on top of it. "Okay, boss."

It was a marvelous spring morning in late April. Who could not be happy on such a day? The air was warm, the sun was bright, the wind a gentle breeze. All the trees on the plaza and ringing the commons were coming into leaf.

"Grady," said Tubby, when he and Judith had come up to him.

Pentecost, concentrating on his flowers, twisted his body and looked up.

"Got somebody here that wants to meet you."

Pentecost pressed the point of the trowel in the ground and stood up. He was taller than Judith expected, and thinner, judging from how his faded bib overalls and threadbare shirt hung off his shoulders.

"This here is the new lady boss of FEFA. Ms. Judith Standard. Been here since last August."

Pentecost turned to her.

She had never seen a more striking face. The high forehead, exceptionally deep-set eyes, flared nostrils, firm lips and bearded chin gave him the look of a prophet or a seer, a Lincoln or a madman.

"I want to thank you—you and your men—for all you do." She held out her hand.

There was a knock on the FEFA door. "My God," said Tubby, "visitors!" He quick-stepped away to meet them.

Pentecost took hold of Judith's hand. A jolt of electricity shot through her.

"The men will 'preciate that."

They dropped hands, and Judith, embarassed, turned to go.

"Saw as you had a poem in *Chestnut*."

Judith turned back to him, startled.

"A good 'un."

"I'm glad you liked it."

"'Cept for one thing."

Judith tried to remain impassive, but she felt her defenses lock into place. "Exactly what thing is that, Mr. Pentecost?"

"Them last two lines. I'd a struck 'em."

Judith almost had. But she had so labored over them she just couldn't bring herself to do so, even if they didn't quite fit. Why hadn't the editor at *Chestnut Review* said something? If this simple groundskeeper could see the error, everybody could! Now the poem was in print, with her name on it.

She poked back. "I've heard you're a poet yourself. Though I wouldn't know."

Pentecost shrugged. "Don't know as one poem

counts."

"One? You've only written *one* poem?"

"Never stops, is all." He knelt down, and with his forefinger pushed aside a mound of the dark mulch, revealing a green shoot, its bloom still sheathed. "So's I keep on writin', like this just keeps on growin'." He stood up again.

Judith stared. "What is this poem?"

Pentecost looked up at her, an unsettling look. "*House of Poetry.*"

Judith felt her skin tingle as she watched Pentecost squeeze one of the small flowers and its rootball out of its pot, opened a seam in the earth, and neatly inserted the plant. He gently pushed in dirt around the flower with both hands. She imagined the roots, pushing quietly through the earth, intertwining with all the roots of everything else. An invisible fabric, a mesh, a skein holding the visible world together. Troubled, she backed away, turned, and walked as steadily as she could to Rare Books.

Tubby had been watching. "Told you he was crazy," he said when she got inside.

Judith tried to laugh.

At her desk in the back room she sat without moving. The books all around seemed to be watching. Was he crazy? Was she? "*House of Poetry,*" she whispered. His house? She couldn't picture him in any house at all. He belonged outside, in the snow and wind, or kneeling on the earth, planting flowers. A bigger house. A world house. Like Wordsworth's Tintern Abbey, open to the sky. This was what she wanted from her own poem. To blow the roof off. Or was this just plagiarism. Appropriating an idea from this mysterious groundsman. But she had taken nothing from him but inspiration. Weren't we all, in the end, bound to awaken to the same truths?

Judith stood up and went back in the lobby and lingered at the window.

Workmen were forking dark mulch from the pickup into wheelbarrows and pushing these to the planted beds at the bookstore, FEFA, and the central oval. They sprinkled the mulch around the flowers. Pentecost stood apart, watching. He turned a little, toward Bertram Hall, and Judith fancied that he was looking into the window of the very office she had once occupied. She felt as if she were being pulled out of that window to float high in the air like a figure in Chagall.

Tubby came up beside her. "To think he came from money," he said, sipping his coffee.

His words were like buckshot, knocking her out of the sky. "What?"

"Money! He came from money."

"What ever do you mean?"

"Why, the Pentecost family is filthy rich. They own swank hotels up and down the East Coast. But ol' G. P. out there walked away from it all. Said he wanted to work in the dirt." Tubby shook his head. "Man! What a nut case."

"Money isn't everything, Tubby," she said, turning on her heel.

"Yeah, but it's way ahead of whatever is in second place!" he called out, as she strode energetically past the bookshelves to her desk in the back room. She sat down and took up her pen. If Judith Standard was ever a poet, she was one then, or thought she was, for she wrote and wrote and wrote, with hardly any revision, or even re-reading, for the rest of the day. Her energy did not abate, but drove her day after day, into the following week, and the weeks beyond that. She missed meals, slept restlessly, forgot things. The only respite was seeing Pentecost on the plaza tending the flowers, pruning trees, mulching beds.

The manuscript pages of her poem piled up. She became possessive of--or possessed by--her work. She wished she'd composed it digitally. Suppose there was a fire in Rare Books. What if a burglar broke in, God forbid? She tucked the pages in a heavy satchel with a shoulder strap. She kept this on her person wherever she went, slept with it under her pillow. It was safe in her locked car. Even then, she found herself reflexively pressing the remote.

Only publication would relieve her of the burden. Once in print her precious poem could never be lost. And she did began to feel, with rising excitement, as summer waned and the trees began to turn color, that she was at last approaching crescendo, whose echoes would never end. She reached out to the publisher of *Chestnut Review*, who referred her to an agent in New York. But send it through the mail? Not before she had a copy. And a backup! Getting this done was complicated and dangerous. There was a copy place downtown. But hand over her precious pages to somebody she didn't know who would take it in a back room out of her sight? Never. She could do it herself: FEFA had a copier. But a few sheets at a time would take forever, and nosy Tubby would figure out she was not doing any proposal, maybe snitch a page and report to somebody. Newsome Library next door had several machines, but they required a special credit card, and the one she had was out of date, which meant she'd have to go over to the Bursar's office to get a new one, etc., etc.

Judith never called the agent. She rushed on toward completion. That was the main thing: completion. One fine fall day on a Friday in October, she was able to write, with an exaggerated flourish, *Finis*. She had imagined this moment many times, and nearly purchased a quill pen and ink well for the purpose. This made her blush. It was enough to stand, stretch, and feel pleased with herself. Hadn't Gibbon, after finishing *The Decline and Fall of the Roman Empire*, taken a "turn in the garden" as celebration? That would be just the thing. She walked straight across the lobby and out the glass doors, heedless of Tubby and his raised eyebrows.

Pentecost and his crew were raking leaves, brown oak and colorful maple, into big piles. At a word from him they broke from their work and went to the pickup, where they sat and talked, nibbled from sandwiches and drank from thermoses. He stood apart, looking toward the Grand Commons, both hands gripping the rake handle.

This was her moment. She walked over to him, willing herself not to rush. She could feel her heart beating. It was all she could do to keep from bursting into speech, to exclaim her poem, her confidence in its power and beauty, and most of all that he had been her inspiration and hoped her confession didn't make him feel uncomfortable. But out here on this public plaza? With students going by, and those idle workers snacking around the truck, and Tubby watching, no doubt? She said nothing.

Pentecost spoke. "Saturday night, I'll be read-in'. From *House*"

"You mean, in front of an audience?"

"Yes, ma'am."

Judith felt a twinge of resentment that he would share his one poem with the public. She had somehow thought it was their private domain, known only to the two of them.

"At the *Ginger Snap*. 'Bout eight. Going to be a poetry slam."

Judith knew the place by reputation. Located on the outskirts of town, it had begun as a church, morphed into a coffee house with an outreach mission of some kind, and gradually deteriorated into a bar and dance floor. Revelers sometimes spilled onto the surrounding fields, leaving behind beer cans and blankets. Hardly the place for a poetry slam, she thought.

"Like to come?"

Was this a date, she wondered? She couldn't bring herself to ask. She had had a bad experience at a place like the *Ginger Snap* in high school. She studied Pentecost. His beard and frayed cap made him look old. But his skin was still smooth, except for wrinkles at the corners of his eyes, and the crease at the bridge of his nose. He did not look dangerous, but you could never tell.

"I might have to work late."

Pentecost nodded, called his men from their break, and returned to work.

He had asked; she vacillated; he turned away. Why was she so timid?

The question festered in her all week. By Saturday, she had resolved to go. What to wear? She laid out all her clothes on the bed, modeled this skirt with that blouse and those shoes. Why? This wasn't a date she was going on. It wasn't anything. Or was it? Never mind all that! This was going to be *her* night out, a personal celebration of poetic accomplishment. Nobody's business but her own. She settled on loose jeans, a pullover blouse, and light wool jacket. Comfortable and inconspicuous.

She pulled into the poorly graded gravel parking lot of the *Ginger Snap* thirty minutes early, sitting in her car until almost eight watching other people, singly or in groups, arrive and go in. She slung the satchel over her shoulder and hurried after them just as the doors were closing. The bar was crowded, and so was the adjoining space, with its ill assortment of folding chairs. People were even standing along the back wall. Up front was a small stage with a microphone and spotlight. She struggled forward and found a lone seat in a middle row. She searched the crowd in vain for Pentecost. She was disappointed but almost pleased. This was not a place he belonged, a thought that made her feel better about herself. Or was he just jerking her chain, like Tubby would do? No! He was too honest for that. Or was he? She berated herself for having come, but with the crowd so dense she could hardly leave without causing a scene.

A young woman with a long ponytail and tattoos on both forearms jumped onto the stage. Garishly illuminated by the spotlight, she took hold of the mic and loudly announced to a pounding of feet that the *10th annual Ginger Snap Poetry Slam* was now open! A heavy-set man in a cowboy hat went first. His cohort of friends cheered when he began and applauded when he ended. He was followed by a wisp of a girl with red hair and a screaming fanbase.

So it went, one aspiring poet after another, in a variety of shapes and sizes and gender identities. Some of their poetry was good, some not. People at the bar got into the act, shouting out doggerel.

The young woman with the ponytail and tattoos hopped on stage. She scanned the room. "Anyone else?" She tapped her beer glass. "Anyone?"

Silence.

"You there!" she called out, pointing at Judith, "you with the mailbag! I'll bet you have a big 'ol poem stuck in there. How 'bout it? Come on up!" The bar people hollered.

Judith wished she could shrivel up and disappear.   She closed her eyes.

"I'll read!"

She opened her eyes.

Grady! Grady Pentecost, in his scuffed boots, faded denim overalls, and thread-bare shirt, with his long-billed cap and pointed wizard's beard glistening in the light stood motionless at the microphone. He wore glasses with large lenses that made him look owl-eyed. Judith decided he was more literate than he let on. The restless audience settled. Even the bar people quieted. From his back pocket Pentecost drew a sheaf of papers, which he sorted and resorted.

Were they unpaginated? Was he lost? Judith began to worry there really was something wrong with him.

He squinted in the spotlight and mumbled into the microphone.

"Speak up, hillbilly!"

Laughter.

"Hell, he cain't read!"

Judith was so furious she jumped to her feet and clapped her hands. "Quiet!"

Somebody yelled at her to sit down, others defended her. The young woman with the ponytail and tattoos intervened.

Pentecost leaned into the microphone. "Been workin' on this awhile."

Judith was relieved. He seemed to be okay. He tugged at the bill of his cap. "May never finish."

More laughter.

"Read the damn thing, hayseed!"

Judith nearly got to her feet again.

"Alrighty then hayseeds and hillbillies," he said.

Juith almost laughed aloud. *Rock the house,* she whispered.

"Listen careful, now."

She did listen, very carefully. But she could make no sense of the rushing river of words, the collapsing wall of syllables. Or maybe she could. A word or two. Here and there, each one a life raft. She clung, she let go, she understood! Then didn't. Then did, almost! She strained to catch the least nuance in his voice . . .

"Fuck this shit!" somebody shouted out.

Cheers, whistles, catcalls. Judith came awake as if from a coma. Music blared; chairs were shoved aside; people danced. Someone crashed into her. She clutched her satchel and struggled through this madness to reach the stage. She must talk to Pentecost.

The microphone had been knocked over and the spotlight turned out. The stage was empty. She rushed around the back curtain and out an exit door.

A light rain was falling, with gusts of chilly wind. "Pentecost!" she called out. "Grady!" She circled the coffee house at an awkward run, the satchel slapping heavily against her thigh. She thought she saw him among cars at the far end of the parking lot, trotted that way, stepped in a hole and pitched forward, the briefcase propelling her fall like a pendulum. She thrust out her hands and fell to her knees, tearing her jeans. She saw in the white glare of a security lamp her bleeding palms.

Cars jockeyed their way out of the rough parking lot, headlights glaring against other cars or into the trees. Judith limped behind a dilapated outbuilding and into a stand of pines where she felt safely hidden. The heavy satchel slipped from her aching shoulder and she began to cry. How she had labored over her work! If labor were merit, surely honor, at least, was her due. If intention were the measure, her poem ought long to be remembered. But neither labor nor intention alone could account for what she had heard that night.

Cold rain pelted her. The lot lights went out. She hoisted the cruel satchel to her shoulder and stumbled in the darkness to her car. Once inside, she pushed the satchel onto the passenger's seat and wiped the rain from her face, tasting blood. Her mind began to clear. "As God is my witness," she said aloud, "and whatever it takes, I am going to get his poem published!" It galled her to think that Tubby said it first, even if mockingly: Pentecost's work deserved a place in her collection of under-represented voices. *House of Poetry* would lead it off. Wouldn't that surprise the President and his staff.

***

By 7:00 am Monday morning, Judith was waiting impatiently at the front windows of FEFA for Pentecost and his crew. She paced. Tubby came in after 9,
late as usual, and fixed himself coffee. She listened to
the clink of his spoon stirring sugar. He took his usual
position by the check-in desk.

"We're awfully anxious today," he said.

"A little."

"Would we like to talk about it, darlin'?"

Judith stopped pacing. "Don't call me that."

He shrugged. "Suit yourself, boss."

She closed her eyes a moment to erase him
from her sight. "Where's Pentecost?"

Tubby sipped noisily. "Guess you didn't hear."

"Hear what?"

"He croaked."

She thrust a finger at him. "Don't you mess
with me."

He grinned. "I ain't. "He kicked the bucket.
Spilled the molasses. Met his Maker."

Judith caught hold of Tubby's arm in both
hands, spilling his coffee. "You're kidding."

"Let go, woman!"
Judith dropped her hands, and Tubby backed away.
"Sunday morning his sister went up to that shack of his
on the mountain. Found him dead as a doornail. Settin'
in his chair. Bottle in his lap."

"Bottle?"

"He was an alkie. Been that for years!"

She struggled with this information. "What
about—his effects?"

Tubby snorted. "*Effects?* Like what? Like I said,

he was a drunk."

"He had papers, *important* papers! What's going to happen to them?"

Tubby nodded toward a man in a dark suit striding across the plaza. "Ask him."

His flippant manner infuriated her. "Get serious."

"I am! That, *dear boss*, is Pentecost's brother. He's a developer and the brains of the outfit."

The man stopped at the oval garden bed, where Judith had watched Pentecost plant flowers. He flicked his cigarette butt into the garden and stepped briskly up to the front door, which Tubby held open for him.

Tall, like Grady, he was clean shaven and smelled of cologne. He wore a gold tie, with a folded kerchief peeking from his vest pocket to match. "I'm looking for a Judith Standard."

Judith stepped forward and held out her hand. "I'm so very sorry for your loss!"

The man touched her hand and let go. "Raymond Pentecost. Executor for the Pentecost estate. I'll get right to the point--."

"Please, before you go on. Your brother was a great poet. I dare say, a *very* great poet. Whitman comes to mind."

"Whitman who."

"*Walt* Whitman, for God's sake!"

"Don't know the man. What is your point?"

Judith tried to meet his eyes. "The point is, I earnestly desire your permission to go through his papers. To preserve and catalogue them for posterity."

Raymond Pentecost held up his hand. "Stop right there. Let me guess. You want to get at *House of*

Poetry. Do I have that about right?"

"Why, yes!"

He took a step closer and bent his head toward her like a predator bird. "For the last fifteen years, when he *should* have been making something of himself, that worthless brother of mine did absolutely nothing, as far as anybody can tell, except grub around with flowers, and fritter his time away on that ridiculous poem of his, or whatever it was. Believe you me, I am sick to death of the thing; me and everyone else in the family."

He stepped back and straightened his tie. "Now I am here in the name of the Pentecost family to settle his debts, dispose of his remains, and build a resort on that property of his. Make some money on it, finally! Which means, for starters, trucking off to the dump every last shred and scrap of his junk."

Judith took hold of his lapels. "You can't!"

"Get your hands off me."

Embarassed, she let go. "I *beg* you. Hold back the trucks for *just* a few hours. I'll get what papers I can. Please!"

Raymond Pentecost smiled, showing crooked teeth. "I love to see a woman beg. But your performance was unnecessary." He drew from the inside pocket of his suit coat an envelope. "Along with the bottle, this was in my brother's miserable hand when he died."

Judith took the envelope, turned it over. "To Judith Standard" was scrawled on the front.

"Open it. I don't have all day."

Carefully, almost reverently, Judith tapped one end of the envelope against her palm and carefully tore off the merest sliver of the opposite end. Squeezing the envelope open, she drew out a stiff paper about the size of a dollar bill. On it was written, in large, bold letters, "ADMIT ONE." Underneath, neatly penned, were the words: *The bearer of this pass is entitled to one night in the House of Poetry.* Below that: "*Compliments of G. Pentecost.*"

Judith ran her finger over his signature as if in doing so she could contact him.

"I give you one night in there," declared Raymond Pentecost. "Bright and early tomorrow morning the bulldozers will begin knocking it all down." He turned smartly on his heel, pushed open the glass doors, and stepped down onto the plaza. At the oval garden he lit a cigarette and tossed the match.

"That resort he's got planned, it'll make money," said Tubby. "I mean to invest. You ought to." He sipped his coffee, eyeing her.

Judith pulled out her phone. "What is the address."

"No way will GPS get you up to Panther's Holler."

The name made her uneasy. She put the phone back in her pocket. "Then give me directions."

"You oughtn't to go up there by yourself, darlin'."

"I'm touched by your concern. How do I get there?"

"Hard-headed, ain't you?"

"I'm waiting."

"You take Main Street all the way out to Cat Mountain Road, bear right, and keep right on a-going 'till the pavement ends. Take the left fork about a mile on, and you'll come to it. You got four wheel drive?"

"No."

Tubby shook his head. "Women!"

By the time Judith got to the end of the pavement on Cat Mountain Road and had started up the rough, winding, left fork gravel road, she was uncomfortably aware that she was in a different world, far removed from the university town where she had lived and worked for twenty years. Now and then she could see in the woods an old, wrecked car, or tumble-down cabin. In a weedy field, ancient farm equipment rusted away. She feared that mountain people were watching her go by. Suppose she got a flat tire? She pictured herself clutching the tire iron like a weapon, as the sun went down and a ragged family of half wits came creeping out of the woods. Of course, that was crazy. Still--. She kept checking the gas gauge. *Why* hadn't she filled up before leaving town?

On and up the road went, bending sharply back and forth, deteriorating as it went. She slowed the car to a crawl, to avoid the worst holes and ruts. There were no more tumble-down cabins up here, no rusty machinery. Just the steep-sided mountains, and the brooding woods all around.

A tree had fallen into the road, and Judith edged the car past, the tires loosening small stones, which bounced noisily out of sight down a sharp dropoff. She came around another sharp bend, and found herself facing a rough rock wall, sporting tufts of fern and glistening with dripping water. She shut off her car, which was covered with dust, turned it back on to make sure it would start, turned it off again. This had to be *Panther's Holler*. She had read that panthers were extinct in this part of the country, but it didn't feel like it, not here. Slowly she got out of the car, quietly shut the door. Gathering herself, she walked away from it, came around the end of the rock wall.

Down from a high ridge, curved like an amphitheatre, spilled long streamers of water in a complicated pattern. Clouds of mist rose where the streamers plunged into deep pools, from which issued sparkling rivulets, joining together along the grassy flat where Judith stood before sluicing through a rocky defile then plunging toward the valley below. The sounds of the water were amplified by the shape of the mountain, and mingled with the flute-like calls of hidden birds.

Then she saw the house. What she took to be a house. Or parts of one. A corner post. A dormer. A windowed tower, its weather vane wreathed in vines. A porch. The door. Everything else was so entwined in greenery and shrouded by trees it was hard to tell where the human architecture ended and nature took over.

She picked her way toward the house, mounted the steps on tiptoe and approached the door. Pinned below a small window was a paper pocket, with neatly printed instructions: *Deposit Ticket Here*. Checking to see if any other tickets had been deposited and finding none, she carefully inserted her own and pushed open the door. Light spilled into a narrow hallway. Torn and crumpled bits of paper, large and small, covered the floor. She bent down, picked one up, and pressed it out flat in her hand: it was covered with markings, a cryptic language, on both sides. She picked up another: more markings. Another: still more.

Judith followed the hallway, which opened into a room. Wan, greenish light filtered through windows which, on their outside surfaces, were a web of leafy vines. The entire room was awash in paper, a waist-high flood of it in the center, swelling up head-high in the corners. Waves of paper bits flowed into the next room. She reached into the sea, plucked out a random paper, and held it to the light. Markings, words, a confusion of both. Front and back. The near wall—nay, every wall—was barnacled with paper bits. Streamers of paper, riffled by a breeze from the open door, dangled from the ceiling.

Judith retreated to the hallway, where the light was better, took off her glasses, and peered at the close writing on a scrap of paper pinned to the wall. She made out *centurion* and further on, *canticle*, followed shortly by a phrase: *While lith I leaf by brookside manor.* Whatever sense resided in these words dissolved into scribbles on adjoining papers, and reassumed the appearance of words on yet other papers. Was this a language? An invented one, like Tolkien's elven tongues? Or German, with its long compound words, carried to the extreme? She followed a line of unbroken characters with her finger, looking for a break. Three—four—five—six feet, and still no end. She broke off, exhausted, her eye settling on a word she recognized: *Ringing.* She felt a pang of happiness, and read the string of words which followed with ease: *Stinging the waters of sumpter she trode.* Then she sat back, puzzled: sense or nonsense? She leaned forward again and resumed deciphering, driven by a feeling of anticipation, even urgency. But there were so many pieces of paper, layered and crowded with words and nonsense lines and syllables and mere scribbles, not written in straight lines, but tracking off in every direction, like diagramming gone mad! She closed her eyes a moment to rest her

     House of Poetry

mind. When she opened them, words of blessed clarity greeted her: WELCOME MY FRIEND, TO THE HOUSE OF POETRY.

Judith stepped back and whooped. Then smiled. She rushed from the house and back to her car. The sun was sinking, its flaming orb briefly impaled upon the needle-sharp tips of the trees at the top of the ridge. She threw open the passenger door, grabbed up the heavy satchel, and hurried back.

Once in the hallway, she turned her beloved satchel upside down, watching delightedly as the sheaves of papers with their painstakingly constructed stanzas spilled like water from a broken dam across the floor. She grabbed up a handful, rushed into the semi-darkness of the next room, and with a shout flung them out over the paper sea, where they fell like a breaking wave.

She got down on her knees and tore willy-nilly at her poem papers with terrific energy, now and then crumpling a page and flinging it like a baseball. She examined a scrap, found a phrase she had liked—*bottling blue ecstacy*—and locating again, with difficulty, WELCOME MY FRIEND, TO THE HOUSE OF POETRY, pushed a corner of the paper up in behind POETRY, so that *bottling blue ecstacy* stuck out at an angle from the word like a strange leaf. She stepped back to evaluate the effect and let out a howl of happiness.

Now she went to work with purpose, even as the light through the door began to drain away. Tearing and fitting, tearing and fitting, Judith dissembled her poem bit by bit, and worked them into the House of Poetry which enclosed and liberated her. At first she worked with great care, first studying the recognizable phrases decaying into hints of other languages which disintegrated into scribbles and mere markings before re-emerging into recognizable words and phrases, and only then fitting her own words and phrases with concentrated precision.

Gradually, as she began to understand, or felt she understood, or would soon understand, if she did not tarry, the underlying meaning of it all, she accelerated. The whole meaning was present, just barely out of reach, if she could only tear and fit fast enough. Overwhelmed by her task, she stopped, near tears, shivering in the chilly evening air. Her fingers were cramping. She rubbed her hands together, closed her eyes, and for an instant distinctly saw her mother sitting with a book at her childhood bedside, and heard her voice: " . . . *but the sparrows implored Peter to exert himself.*"

The spell vanished, and with renewed energy Judith worked her way up the staircase, tearing and fitting, tearing and fitting in utter silence except for the paper noise, and now in almost complete darkness. Coming to the top step, she was surprised to see a thin band of pale light streaming out from under a door. She forgot the papers in her hand, which cascaded to the floor, took a quiet step forward and opened the door. Bright moonlight washed over her and she shaded her eyes, slowly seeing that she was in a library, with books from floor to ceiling on every wall and the windowed tower overhead. There was not a scrap of paper on the floor, nor anywhere else. The only furniture, in the very center of the room, was a small table and overstuffed chair. Someone sat in the chair. Someone with a long pointed beard and the profile of a madman or a proph-

 House of Poetry

et, staring up into the moonlight. Someone dressed in scuffed boots, frayed denim overalls, and a threadbare shirt.

Judith gasped. Had Pentecost's sister, finding him dead two nights ago, actually decided to just leave his body where it was? Or was he not dead? Was this an elaborate ruse to get her here, all alone, in this dark house, high on a lonely mountain?

Frightened, Judith felt in her pockets for a weapon. Her fingers found nothing but a hairpin. She took a slow-motion, noiseless step forward. Another. "Pentecost?" she asked in a trembling voice.

She dared another step.

"Grady?"

No response.

His exceptionally deep-set eyes were open, and his mouth. His skin was pallid, almost pearly in the moonlight. His chest did not rise or fall. A large book lay open in his lap.

Stretching out her hand with infinite care, she touched his arm at the bony wrist, just below the sleeve. The thumb and forefinger of his hand parted ever so slightly, releasing a torn paper, which fluttered to the floor at her feet. Its words stared up at her: "Poetry! We're makin' poetry--" Judith didn't know whether to laugh or weep; she was tempted to bend forward and kiss him, but saw to her horror a tiny ant climbing his beard. She bolted from the room and plunged headlong down the stairs. In the darkness she missed a step and fell hard, striking her head and blacking out.

***

Judith was roused by a tremor, which at first she thought was inside her, and then wakened by a headache. She opened her eyes; sunlight was flooding through the front door. She raised a hand to her temple and felt the bulge. Another tremor dizzied her; she gripped the bannister. A piece of plaster fell from the ceiling, struck the bannister, and exploded into shrapnel. She felt the floor trembling.

Judith struggled to her feet and burst onto the front porch. Trucks and wrecking machines were moving heavily and noisily into position. A bulldozer, its metal treads clanking, was backing down off a trailer.

Pillage! Sacrilege! Madness! She yelled obscenities; heedless, the heaviest bulldozer set its course, clanking and grinding its way toward her, pushing down small trees as it came, rocks splintering. With his hands upon the controls, the operator, a cigarette clenched in his teeth and hardhat set at a jaunty angle, squared his blade to the front steps and settled in for the last few yards before impact.

Judith Standard braced for destruction. For a visionary moment she saw all: the 'dozer crash into the steps, the porch crushing inward, corner posts snapping, windows shattering, walls collapsing, the windowed tower breaking loose, plunging downward, dragging trees and vines with it, ragged pieces caught in vine ropes twanging upwards in clouds of dust and debris, bits of paper poetry floating away or caught in branches. Steel jaws biting into and breaking clapboard siding and wall timbers, some with papers and their scribbles pinched together and stuck on nails; the confused jumble cascading down into noisy, lumbering dump trucks with tremendous crash and buckle, as

     House of Poetry

dust, debris, paper scraps go spinning up into the air. Chains banging dented tailgates and puffing acrid blue diesel smoke, the trucks go rattling, bumping, banging down the mountain, debris slipping off the sides, a board with shingles clinging to it, poetry papers stuck to the nails, to crash against tree trunks, rotting there for decades. On to the dump go the heavy trucks loaded with the mangled heaps of the House of Poetry, where sea gulls rise in clouds, the trucks backing up and dumping, gigantic muddy equipment moving in to crush it all into the mud and heaps of other garbage, papers stuck to the bulldozer tracks, gulls rising and settling, picking at food scraps, all the massively entangled garbage and scribbled paper bits flattened and trampled, covered with dirt, the whole process repeated day after day, week after week, month after month, year upon year, compacted into seeping, fetid earth, dense, rank, sodden, as tiny creatures by the billions chew, digest, fart the poetry and debris into gas bubbling in tiny bubbles up, up to the surface again decades and even generations later when the dump is closed and forgotten, the gas to rise like spirits, hugging the air as likewise downward are pressed poetry scraps saturated with leaching fluids from shingles, wood, old oil cans, broken sump pumps, erasers, tabletops, the infinitude of our treasured or discarded belongings, leaching darkly together through underground runnels, finding their sly way, to join the earth's waters in cavernous underground limestone caves, or seeping somewhere out into a farmer's field, where the cows gravely graze. Creeks going to rivers, rivers to the sea, the House of Poetry and its scribbled papers now the rippling blueness of oceans, evaporating into the hot atmosphere to become acid rain killing the trees, even those trees on the ridgetop of Panther's Holler, as the earth turns and the sun shines, and we celebrate or protest, and die withal until centuries hence, extinction again, our species gone. How could that be, the Blue Planet gone gray, while the flaming sun goes on flaming until the heat at last registers into sea-wigglings, and up rises life again, swimming, leaping, flying, assertive, the long ages watching expectantly the unhurried progression upwards into the history of our race again, or another, hunting and building their way from forests into houses and streets, the complexity of warfare and the arts, writing and civilization, and the preservation of the artifacts of civilization, and poetry, the blessed House of Poetry, in which we all live, desperately and in pleasure until the final trumpet when this moment arrives again in splendor and collapse. Again and again and again.

Reeling from her vision, Judith came half way down the front steps, staring in wonder at the bulldozer. The operator throttled down his machine and waved her to get off the porch. She stood her ground, grinning. "Poetry!" she yelled exultantly, thrusting her arms in the air, "we're makin' poetry!"

The son of a literature professor and a grade school librarian, **Lawrence Bechtel** received his B.A. from Wheaton College and M.A. from Virginia Tech, where he taught English and wrote his first novel. In 1989, he took up sculpture, which eventually led to public and private commissions, including "Officer Down" and "Calling the Powers" in Roanoke. In 1992, Bechtel became Virginia Tech's first Recycling Coordinator (and Solid Waste Manager), a position from which he retired in 2009. An opportunity to sculpt a portrait bust of Thomas Jefferson led to a portrait bust of Isaac Granger, who became the protagonist in his *Tinsmith's Apprentice* historical fiction trilogy. The first volume, *A Partial Sun*, was published in 2019, the second, *That Dazzling Sun*, in 2020. Lawrence is at work on the third, *A Slow Eclipse*.